Thursdays in the Park

A Collection of
Short Stories and Poems

Compiled by
the Creative Writing Group
of
Maple Leaf Golf & Country Club
Port Charlotte, Florida

Edited by
Walter Lemon

LCCN: 2012946569
ISBN: 978-0-9859504-1-5
First edition, published 2012.

Ward Bitz Publishing
Baldwinsville, NY

The editor may be contacted at:
2100 Kings Highway, Lot 437
Port Charlotte, FL 33980
941-391-6853
walterlemon@rogers.com.

Introduction

This book is a sample of the short stories and poems produced by past and present participants in the Maple Leaf Golf & Country Club Creative Writing Group. The purpose is to provide some history of the park and our group, plus raise money to donate to local charities. The participants value the strong sense of community at Maple Leaf and the opportunity to share their writing interests with their fellow residents.

The leadership of John Wright and the guidance of Bob Bitz, who has published five books already, were instrumental in the development of the book. Thank you to all Writing Group participants for selflessly providing materials for inclusion, and to Sue Dwyer, Walt Lemon and Bill O'Hare for assembling the Writer's stories, editing and reporting historical materials. We trust that the residents of Maple Leaf and their families and friends will enjoy reading our material.

Cover photo of nature scenes courtesy of Bill McGee.
Aerial photos courtesy of John Bradley.
MLG&CC scenes courtesy of Bob Bitz.

A Heavenly Place
by Wilma Angus

Did you ever hear our Park called,
    a heavenly waiting room?
that we're just a bunch of old fogies
    down here taking up room.
Well, I'm not waiting around to be called
    to that heavenly home on high.
I'm living it up with dancing and singing
    and everything else I can try.
We've put in our stint of helping mankind
    twenty five – thirty years, I'd say.
We no longer spend eighty hours on the job,
    we're spending that time at play.
There's Bocce, Lawn Bowling and Shuffle Board,
    enjoyed every day of the week.
There's something new to be learnt each year,
    there's classes, any topic you'd seek.
We've been turned out to pasture, they say,
    are we no longer of any use.
Ask the volunteers that go out every day
    to the hospitals, churches and schools.
We all pull together to improve our Park,
    volunteering for this and that.
Look after each other through Neighbors on Call.
    Teaching each others our crafts.

There's joggers and walkers and riding bikes
　　and who can forget about golf.
Still improving my slice and once in a while,
　　A hole in one is pulled off.
Are we too old to plan for next year?
　　do we feel our life's in the past?
Is there nothing for us to look forwards to?
　　Is next year too much to ask?
I answer with an astounding NO.
　　We'll watch for each new invention.
Our computer classes are all filled up.
　　Keeping up with the new generation.
So we all sail off in this brand new year,
　　a brand new century.
I'm anxious to see what it holds in store,
　　for myself and others like me
There's so much going on in our little Park,
　　to list them would take all night.
If this really is Heaven's waiting room,
　　it's a Heavenly place all right.

Table of Contents

Dedication

This book is dedicated to John Wright, who has led the Maple Leaf Creative Writing Group for the past 10 plus years. John brings wisdom, knowledge and flair to all our meetings, and uses humour to accentuate his positive feedback. John has worked tirelessly to raise the level of our collective writing abilities, and his energy and enthusiasm show in the work contained herein. John, on behalf of all past and current participants in the Maple Leaf Creative Writing Group, we offer our heartfelt thanks and warmest appreciation for all your wonderful leadership. We wish you many more years of writing and we look forward to your continued leadership.

Creative Writing Group – Some History
Helping Seniors to Write Gooder

The Creative Writing Group was initially founded approximately 1991, with Wally Frazer as the original leader. Current participants Al and Lorna Hamilton were among the early writers in training. The purpose in the early days was to bring together like-minded residents who wanted to improve their writing skills. Some of the early participants, as well as probably most of us who have joined the group since, were interested in writing family history, or felt that they had a book bottled up inside them. In conjunction with leading the group, Wally published a book about his experiences as a Liberator bomber pilot in WWII, titled *A Trepid Aviator.*

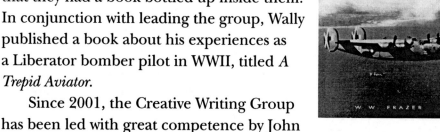

Since 2001, the Creative Writing Group has been led with great competence by John Wright. As you might imagine, it is never easy to keep ten to fifteen writers with egos and stories to tell focused on the essentials of the group. The main tenets of the group are:

- Learn how to set up and create your story
- Discover ways to build suspense, dialogue and effective story lines
- Share your stories with your peers
- Learn proper punctuation and spacing

Some of the books published by participants

The process as developed by Wally Frazer so many years ago, and refined by John, is that each writer prepares a 500 word story each week, prints out sufficient copies of his or her story for all attendees, distributes them and then reads his or her story aloud. At the end of the reading, the participants are requested to provide feedback and critique. One of the challenges for John in today's environment is to keep the discussion focused. Many of us relate to the stories we have just heard and often want to incorporate our personal experiences to the writer's story. John is particularly adept at find the learning points in someone's story. It may be an unusual use of a word or phrase, or it might be an inadvertent change of tense, or the employment of terminology that might not be known to the casual reader. He reminds us that we must write to our audience, and if we neglect to do this, we may leave them misunderstanding or not appreciating our story.

Poetry is perhaps not as widespread as prose among our writers, but there are some tremendous examples contained in this book of both forms of writing. Those of us who do not seem to be able to rhyme two sentences marvel at the wonderful poems that some of our writers produce. Among the prose, the reader will find family histories, serious and inane happenings in our lives, some science fiction, military and work related stories, and just plain funny articles.

Most of our gatherings are full of laughter and interesting comments, along with the occasional tear when a story is especially heart-rending. If you were to ask any of the participants, everyone would comment on the challenges of writing that weekly epistle, but more likely, you would hear about the sheer enjoyment of each weekly session and that we treasure the great friendships we have built through our participation.

The group is very diverse in age, origins, interests and writing styles. Those factors all contribute to the subject matter, the styles of presentation, the experiences being shared, and the different types of humour and the use of colloquialisms. We welcome visitors

Chris Vaughan, Larry Coglan, Sue Dwyer, John Wright, Ralph Woolverton, Wilma Angus, Phyllis Poirier

John Wright, Ralph Woolverton, JJ Alexander, Lorna Hamilton, Phyllis Poirier, Sue Dwyer, Larry Coglan

Marj Behnfeldt, Walt Lemon, Jean Wright, Chris Vaughan, Wilma Angus

to come and listen to our stories, with a view to recruiting new members into our activity. We meet every Thursday morning from November through March, 9:00 to 11:00 in the library.

In 2008, Brenda, the widow of the late Phil Harte donated an award in Phil's name, with the inscription 'In living memory of Phil Harte. In life, Phil made everyone he knew feel special. In death, he continues to urge us to follow our dreams'. Phil was a regular member of the group, and as John Wright relates "Phil invariably ended every meeting with the statement – that has to be the best meeting we have ever had." The Phil Harte Award is given to the person who makes the most significant contribution to the well-being of the Creative Writing Group. Joanne (JJ) Alexander assisted in the creation of the award. The initial recipients were:

2008 – 2009   JJ Alexander – For her generous spirit
2009 – 2010   Sue Dwyer – For three separate reasons
2010 – 2011   John Wright – For his leadership
2011 – 2012   Walt Lemon – Our 'Book Man'

Bill O'Hare, Maxine Stocker, Guy Crombie

For many years, the group has held a pot-luck dinner to celebrate end-of-season, another of our cherished opportunities to meet, except this one includes spouses. Sally and Jim Shirley hosted this event for many years.

Many of the writers have honed their skills to the point that they have published one or more books, or have entered their stories to literary workshops. The true rewards, however, are the skills we have built, the friendships we have forged, and the good times we experience through our writing.

A Brief History of
Maple Leaf Golf and Country Club

As we prepare this book in the spring of 2012, some updating of park history is required. Today, Maple Leaf Golf and Country Club (MLG&CC) is a 55-plus gated community with approximately 1,100 homes and 1,800 residents during the winter. For the 15th year in sequence, the residents of Charlotte County have voted MLG&CC the 'Best Manufactured Home Community'. About 250 'rounders' are proud to call Maple Leaf their year-round home, and love the quiet times when the snow-birds head north for the summers. The sense of community is very strong, with about 50% of the residents from the USA and most of the remainder from Canada. In searching the directory, there are residents who list their home addresses from 28 states and 7 provinces respectively, with the longest commuters coming from Alaska, Calgary and Newfoundland. In addition, there are a few families from England, Norway, Switzerland and Germany. Diversity is wonderful and everyone adds to the character of MLG&CC as they participate in the many activities available.

In 1996 the Park published a book written by Gordon M. Ward titled *A History of Maple Leaf Estates – A Mobile Home Community at Port Charlotte, Florida, 1976 – 1995*. This is an excellent reference document for those interested in the origins and the first 20 years of Maple Leaf. It is not our intent here to reproduce all the information in that reference, but to provide a brief summary of those 20 years and then to provide some perspective on the ensuing 16 years, 1996 – 2011.

The Canadian development firm Baycrest Consolidated Holdings Ltd. based in Mississauga, Ontario, Canada acquired 285 acres of land covered with tropical vegetation and the ten-acre McCready Lake. Maple Leaf Estates Inc. was incorporated under Florida State laws with the Certificate of Incorporation dated January 20, 1976. Murray Ross (VP of Baycrest) was named the first President of Maple Leaf Estates and Robert Harrison was named Resident Manager. Previously, Harrison had owned and operated a mobile home sales company for 25 years in Venice, Florida. The official opening of the park was held on Saturday, July 17, 1976 at 11:45 a.m.

The early sales promotion included advertising in the provinces of Manitoba, Ontario, Nova Scotia, New Brunswick and Quebec, plus the states of Florida, Indiana, Illinois, Michigan and Ohio, aimed at middle aged and middle-income families approaching retirement. When they had sufficient interested customers, they would fly them to Maple Leaf to inspect the park before buying.

Construction began and continued at a brisk pace, with the Queensway surfaced as far as the CanAm clubhouse. The tennis courts had been built by mid-1976, along with a heated swimming pool, a shuffle board court and a large fishing dock on the lake with had been stocked with fish. All the streets were given Canadian names. The second recreational facility was the Country Club building in 1977. By 1980, 890 lots were complete with services. In 1981, a new clubhouse called the Queensway Center was opened and the Sandbar was built on the covered veranda of the Country Club.

An 18-hole Executive Golf Course was a principal feature of Maple Leaf promotion, and clearing of the land began in May 1977. The architect was Layne Marshall of Sarasota. The first nine holes were opened in February 1978, with the full course in play on June 1, 1981.

When the Maple Leaf Homeowner's Association was formed in 1977, it was decided to publish a monthly Newsletter. The first edition called Accents came out in December 1980 and continues to this day.

In the course of time since 1976, the Park has had eight Managers, with current General Manager John Bradley having the longest tenure, 1993 to the present.

In 1980 Baycrest went into receivership and Maple Leaf Estates Inc. was purchased by Herb Stricker, President of Heathcliffe Developments Ltd., a Canadian company, in partnership with Meridain Building Group of Toronto, for approximately $8.5 million. Mr. Stricker was a home owner in Maple Leaf who saw the future potential of the park. In June 1986, Hugh Keith bought Maple Leaf Mobile Home Park (plus Rampart Utilities) for $14 million. By 1989, it became apparent that Mr. Keith was unable to fulfill his financial obligations. A M.L.E. Homeowners' Corporation meeting was held in Punta Gorda on March 20, 1990, and the approval was given to the Board to proceed. The sale was completed on May 1st, 1990 for $22 million.

For the period 1990 to 1995, the following acted as Corporation President:

- *Jerome McHale*
- *Harold Blake*
- *Neil McNabnay*
- *Stuart Rees*
- *Robert Faulkner*

Louise Briggs acted as the Corporate Secretary for this period.

All of the preceding material is from the original History Book written by Mr. Ward and we acknowledge the value of this significant research. We encourage any homeowner who wishes to know more about the early days of Maple Leaf to borrow a copy from one of their neighbours. Many long time residents have their personal copies.

As we begin to develop a brief history of Maple Leaf going forward from 1995, we are indebted to the following for their input, stories, recollections and research: Ralph Woolverton, John Bradley and many acquaintances.

Hurricane Charley hit MLG&CC on August 13, 2004 with devastating effects not only to Maple Leaf but also to the communities of Port Charlotte and Punta Gorda. In MLG&CC,

approximately half the homes were destroyed to the extent that they had to be replaced, with another 25% or more of the homes requiring extensive repairs. The Queensway Centre was heavily damaged, and required major renovations. Emergency response groups took control of the park to ensure that there were no residents trapped in their homes, to safeguard the properties and to maintain order. Some residents to this day felt that some of the damage was caused by emergency response staff, as they entered every home, regardless of damage. To do this, they sometimes knocked down doors or punched holes in windows. As a result, many homes that had not suffered storm damage endured water damage from doors or windows broken by staff. One long time resident reported seeing a piece of two-by-four wood that had been propelled through an exterior wall, then punctured an interior wall and ended imbedded in the other exterior wall. What a force of nature to do that! Other residents who hurried down to Maple Leaf from their summer homes were amazed at the sights: pieces of walls and roofs littering all the roads and hanging from the trees, trees smashed and toppled, aluminium and steel floating in the ponds. There were roofs torn off, with carports and lanai remnants scattered everywhere. It was a tragedy, but MLC&CC recovered, rebuilt and moved on. Unfortunately, the park lost some older residents who could not bear the pain of rebuilding. On the other hand, new residents bought homes and rebuilt, the park was rejuvenated and revitalized to the pleasant and welcoming community it is today.

The following provides some MLG&CC personal perspectives of long-time resident, Ralph Woolverton, who purchased in 1979.

"Dorothy and I were living in Thunder Bay in 1979. We saw a notice in the local paper about a seminar to be given in a local hotel about a new mobile home park in Florida. It was the coldest evening in the winter. We drove in from our country home, arriving too late to get the brochure. I think we were the only ones out of the hundred or so attendees that eventually bought in MLE.

We came to Florida on a 'fly-down' to inspect the development around March 1, 1979. There were about 50 people on the chartered aircraft, leaving Toronto on a Friday afternoon, and returning on the Sunday evening. It was raining when we got here and the air was warm and humid. Joyce and Ralph McDowell from Ottawa were on the flight. Joyce is still in the park, remarried to Glenn Michael. Mr. Harrison was the general manager and chief salesman. We were wined and dined throughout the weekend, with a barbeque at the Peace River Park on Saturday afternoon.

We signed up for a Niagara model, priced at $29,000 US. The Canadian dollar at that time was 93 cents. We were told the house would be ready by October that year. It was to be on lot #571, a perimeter lot where JJ Alexander now resides. The paved road, the Queensway ended at the entrance to Selkirk Lane. The Queensway Centre was just being planned. The sales office was in the house at 498 Trillium. We stayed in the house at 434 Trillium, the same model as we had eventually decided to buy. All of Victoria Court was model homes. I still have some of the plans and specifications for the various homes we inspected.

In May, Mr. Harrison phoned us and said they could not fit the house we had picked out on lot #571, but we could choose any other lot in the vicinity to place the house, the lot rental would remain the same. So we ended up on a Prime Interior corner lot at a perimeter lot rental (#576).

In August we were told that the house was finished, and we could fly down to close the deal and occupy the house. When we arrived in mid-September we found the house was not finished – the lanai and carport had not been built and the landscaping had not been started. We did not close, and went home disappointed. We did order the basic furniture for the house from the furniture store that was set up in the park. When we drove back down in December, the house was completed to our satisfaction, so we closed the deal and the lot rent started on January 1, 1980. The house was the first in the area, and it was surrounded by a sand and gravel desert. The Queensway was still under construction and could be seen from our house. Over the years since we have witnessed all the development around us. The last house to move into the park was on lot #572.

We visited for a week in August of 1982. I came in from South America and Dorothy came down from Ottawa. When we drove into the park, we found it in disarray. The grass was knee-high, the shrubbery was untrimmed, and it was a disaster. It went into receivership – no one would deliver anything to the park unless they had cash or a certified check. The Canadian Imperial Bank of Commerce (CIBC) now owned the property. Every single lot was resurveyed. Mr. Stricker bought it from the CIBC for $8.5 million US dollars. He later sold it to Hugh Keith, a Miami developer, for approximately $14 million US dollars. Many people thought that Mr. Keith was the 'second coming', as he boasted about what he was going to do for the park. He invited residents to invest in his company, and several residents did so. However, some of us thought he may have been running a 'ponzi scheme'.

Many services that were promised in the early days of the park were never to be. There was to be a daily bus that took residents downtown to the Promenades Mall and back. There was a covered boathouse on the main lake, where the cenotaph is now, where residents could store their boats and canoes. We could paddle our canoes on the main lake. At one time there were paddle boats that we were able to enjoy with visitors. One year there was a water ski show on the lake, paid for, probably, by Mr. Keith. Another year there was 'Thanks Hugh' day in the park, with free barbecued hot dogs, and beer. Rampart Utilities operated the sewerage plant located within the park. It was continually breaking down, sending foul odours throughout the park. It was included in the sales of the park until Mr Keith sold the park to the residents in 1990, when it was kept out of the deal as a separate operating company, and eventually acquired by Charlotte County Utilities.

Hurricane Charlie in 2004 changed the park in many ways. About 1/3 of the houses were destroyed, and removed. Many long-time residents never returned to rebuild or replace their houses. This made room for new homes and new people. The new houses were bigger, taller, and much more expensive. The percentage of Canadian owners has decreased to about 50%. Many new residents are from northern states, or live here permanently (the rounders). We live here in harmony, enjoying the life style, taking part in many activities and keeping young! The park is on good financial grounds, and will provide a winter haven for 'Snowbirds 'for many more years!'

Anatomy of a Hurricane

by John Bradley

I speak from firsthand knowledge since I stayed in the park during the hurricane. We had so many residents that had no time to evacuate and there was no time for mandatory evacuation due to the projected path of the hurricane.

On Friday, August 13, Tropical Storm Charley was off south Florida and it was still expected to stay off the coast and impact between Venice and Tampa. We knew our buildings were not constructed for a category 3 or 4 storm, but it was too late for the county to order a mandatory evacuation. Our staff made final preparations and homeowners begin to fill the CanAm and Queensway buildings. We released our staff in late morning to go and secure their own homes. Two of our maintenance workers volunteered to stay in the buildings to run generators and assist homeowners. A sales staff member/homeowner agreed to be the coordinator in the Queensway clubhouse, and also work the radio that was to become our only communications between the two buildings. I would manage operations from the CanAm clubhouse. A few homeowners wouldn't leave their pets at home and we made a decision to bring pets into the CanAm so the homeowners would come to the shelter. We put owners with dogs in the billiard room and owners with cats and birds in the library. We made a decision to position a tractor near the park entrance in case we could not get to the maintenance area after the storm. By early afternoon there were indications that the hurricane could turn east towards Charlotte Harbor and it was upgraded to a category 4. Final coordination was made between staff at the CanAm and Queensway and briefings were provided to homeowners in each building. All were reminded that when the eye passes over, it may feel that the storm has passed, but no storm shutters should be opened because the back side of the storm will begin soon. There were about 250 persons in the two clubhouses. Members of Port Charlotte Village frantically came to MLE to share our shelters. The Holiday Inn was evacuated in Punta Gorda and many of their residents also came to the CanAm.

Feeder bands began to buffet us and the full force of the hurricane hit shortly after 4 pm. The roofing could be heard separating from the two clubhouse shelters and water began leaking into parts of both buildings. The noise from the force of the wind and rain as well as the parts of mobile homes hitting the two buildings was tremendous. During the worst part of the initial eye wall, there was a banging on the shelter doors of the CanAm. It was two homeowners who had elected to stay at their home near the CanAm, but had now decided they needed to get to the shelter. We could not open the shelter doors, because we would probably have lost the entire building if the wind had been able to get inside. The kitchen door of the CanAm as downwind at the time, and by yelling at them to go to that door together with a maintenance worker going outside to escort them, they got inside. As the roof and ceiling separated at the east end of the CanAm, where the billiard room and library are, we had to put everyone in the main room, including the dogs, cats, and birds. As the trees toppled, one came down on the generator for the CanAm. The homeowners and guests who rode this out at the two clubhouses experienced something I am sure they will never forget. The eye wall did pass directly over us and it became very still and quiet; bright light was evident through the slat cracks in the storm shutters. Then the next eye wall arrived, with the wind coming from the opposite direction, now the west. What followed were many feeder bands and we finally opened some doors for everyone to look out just before dark, or about 8 pm. There were damaged homes everywhere, including pieces of homes in the tops of trees. No roads were passable and many were under water. The maintenance man, Mark and I were able to reach the Queensway by about 10:00 pm, but we had maintained radio contact throughout the storm. At about midnight, a thunderstorm hit. All those in the shelter remained there all night.

Saturday, August 14, many staff members showed up, even some who had lost their own homes. Since we had prepositioned the tractor near the gate, a path was made down the Queensway the width of the tractor. This would permit some access as well as get emergency vehicles in. Then the maintenance staff started to work side streets. We had no power or water and wouldn't for a month. A command post was established in the west end of the CanAm. Some relatives showed up to take some of those residents who had stayed. It was reported that over 9,000 homes in the county are destroyed. Over 2,000 National Guard and 400 law enforcement personnel headed for the area. Florida Light and Power (FLP) amassed a force of over 4,000 utility repairmen from as far away as Minnesota. An alternate county command post was established in the Winn-Dixie parking lot, since much of the main command post at the airport was destroyed. Water began to be made available at the county command post. Since there is no power in the county, there is no fuel. A curfew from 8 pm to 7 am was implemented. Most homeowners who rode out the storm in the clubhouses remained in the clubhouses for a second night.

Sunday, August 15 saw more emergency and other assistance vehicles arriving in the park. The Red Cross began to deliver food. Church groups arrived with water, food, and assistance to clean debris. A fleet of county school buses arrived to take homeowners to a Red Cross shelter established at Ainger Middle School in Englewood. Most homeowners went, but some wanted to stay in our shelter. We agreed, but only for another night or so, since health issues were a problem without facilities. Staff from the National Guard and the Miami-Dade police department began to patrol the park. Over 80,000 county residents were still without power. Our staff continued to clear roads and to get equipment operational, as well as clear debris. The park command post was manned by staff and volunteers 7 days a week.

On Monday, August 16, 70,000 were still without power in the county. Rescue units from Palm Beach and Fort Lauderdale arrived and began going house to house in the park to check for casualties. Power was finally restored to local hospitals.

Tuesday, August 17, 66,000 people were still without power in the county. Hundreds of trucks began arriving in county for debris removal.

On Wednesday, August 18, 62,000 were still without power. A 250 pound black bear was caught roaming through Punta Gorda Isles.

Thursday, August 19, 54,000 were still without power in the county.

In the days and weeks that followed so much happened it would take too long to review. One of the events was a homeowner sending nine generators from Canada to provide us with power. The immigration/customs official at the Canada-U.S. border called me on my cell phone to confirm that he should let the shipment enter the U.S.

In discussions with Wayne Sallade, Director of Emergency Management, he indicated that data showed that we not only had winds in excess of 145 mph, but there were gusts to 190 mph. The data may result in the storm being re-categorized as a 5. Whatever the results, the fact remains that Maple Leaf was in the middle of one of the strongest hurricanes ever to hit the United States.

Courtesy of John Bradley, General Manager, MLG&CC.

Current Activities in MLG&CC

In the spring of 2012, there are almost 100 different activities for residents and renters to savour, from golf to tennis, lawn bowling, bocce, all manner of card games, swimming, exercise, word-working, shuffleboard, darts, mini-golf, ceramics, drawing, painting, writing and many, many others. Many residents participate in a wide range of these activities. The Golf and Tennis Associations run a number of competitive events for residents, plus the Tennis Club has teams that participate in local competitive leagues. In addition, there is a constant stream of social events, from dinner dances to block parties, to guest entertainers, to informal get-togethers. Some of the more prominent events are Rally for The Cure Golf Tournament, The Merrymakers, Celebrity Series, Arts and Crafts Show, Strawberry Social, The Woodworkers Dinner Dance, Valentine's Dance, St. Patrick's Day Dance, Parade of Carts and many, many more.

The major venues seem to be busy every day and every hour of the week. As a result, residents have a wealth of opportunities to meet their neighbours and friends, to partake in social and sporting activities, or to just relax at one of the three pools and spas. Many find time to work out in the fully equipped gym, or work on their computer skills at the Computer Club, or to walk or cycle around the part. Constant participation or activity seems to be on the agenda of many residents. Others use the library to find the reading they prefer to merely relax with a good book.

For the period 1996 to 2012, the following acted as Corporation President:

Robert Faulkner	1996 – 1998
E.A. (Ted) Smith	1998 – 2000
Robert Santin	2000 – 2002
Donald Wollstein	2002 – 2003
Garry Weimer	2003 – 2004
Bill Charlton	2004 – 2005
Bernie Derencin	2005 – 2006
John Gonsalves	2006 – 2007
Robert Moore	2007 – 2009
Keith McGruer	2009 – 2010
Richard Hall	2010 – 2012
William O'Hare	2012 –

And now, enjoy our short stories.

WILMA ANGUS

I was born in 1924 in the foot hills of eastern Pennsylvania and spent sixty five years of my life there. Graduated from Bloomsburg High School in 1942, was a teenager through WWII. Married a farmer and had five children, divorced and came to Florida where I married my high school sweet heart.

Number 3

Number three, what do you do with number three? First you have your little boy to follow in his father's footsteps. Bright, energetic and lovable. Then your little girl to help Mother around the house. But what do you do with number three, especially if it is a girl, a pale ordinary girl that seems to always be in the way. To go to a restaurant, four is the perfect number, what do you do with the odd one?

You go shopping, you hold the hands of one on each side, and what do you do with the odd one? What do you do with number three?

Then along comes number four, well, the family is all wrong anyway, maybe this one will be another son. You can always use another son. But no, it's another girl. Yeah, but what a girl, beautiful, lots of dark curly hair and sparkling eyes, precocious and so cute. Now I know what to do with number three, she can look after this treasure.

So number three, named Carol, soon learned that if that treasure, named Jewel, got hurt or into trouble, she was punished. Of course it was her fault as that was her job, to take care of her. And so they grew up, Jewel, beautiful, the pride of the family. Carol, plain, ignored as an ugly, unwanted thing.

Suddenly Jewel is thirteen and found the boys who all love her, but Daddy is suddenly very protective, she's too young but Mommy doesn't think so, so they compromise. She can go if Carol goes and looks after her. Now everyone knows that just doesn't work. Carol doesn't want to tag along and Jewel doesn't want her there. The simple solution is soon found, Carol goes to the library till Jewel comes for her to go home.

Boys, plural, soon dribbles down to one boy who comes to the house real often, so it does work out good till he goes off to war. Jewel is suddenly without someone at her beck and call. She likes to flirt and be the center of attention. So when the local collage became a training center for Navy Cadets she found herself in a virtual paradise. A simple errand to the store became a big adventure. She suddenly was going out every night she was allowed. It was simple to ask who ever to bring along a friend for her sister because she wasn't allowed to go without her.

Carol hated seeing the look in their eyes when they saw her, they would look at Jewel and then at her but it was soon alright because Jewel soon had them both laughing and enjoying themselves while Carol walked along and was quiet.

Jewel was finagling around more and more so that she could go alone and that suited Carol a lot, she didn't want to go. So it was no surprise that she had a date tonight to go alone. What was the surprise was that she made Mommy angry. Maybe Mommy was having a bad day because she never got angry at Jewel or if she did, soon got over it. This time was different. Jewel forgot herself and sassed Mommy back. Mommy said she had to stay home that night. Jewel said she couldn't do that as it wouldn't be fair to the Cadet. We had no telephone or any way to let him know. She argued with Mommy but it did no good.

Mommy at least thought it over, you could hear her mumbling to herself, all he wanted was someone to go to the movies with him. He was away from home and lonesome and wanted someone to talk with. Well, at last she made a decision, if that was all he wanted, Carol could go instead.

Jewel just gasped when Mommy told us her decision. Carol and Jewel both knew that wouldn't do but Mommy wouldn't listen to them.

So after dinner Carol had to go get dressed up and be ready when he arrived. Mommy was all ready for him when he knocked.

"Jewel is being punished and can't go tonight." Mommy is quick to explain.

"Oh, I'm sorry." he answered and turned to leave, Mommy caught him by the sleeve.

"Since you just want company to go to the movies with you, her sister will go instead."

He saw me standing them embarrassed. "That won't be necessary," he answered.

Mommy grabbed me by the arm and pushed me out the door at him. He stepped aside, looked at Mommy and then at me. Took my arm and started walking up the street with me.

I was so embarrassed, I didn't say anything till we were up around the corner, not even tell him my name when he had asked. Out of sight of the house and neighbors, I stopped, turned to him and said.

"I know I'm not Jewel, no one wants me instead of her. I'm sorry Mommy did what she did. I won't embarrass you in front of your friends. I'll go down to the library and read till it's time to go home."

"Oh, no. you'll do no such thing. I wouldn't hear of it."

"I do it all the time. Jewel doesn't want me with her. It's a simple solution."

"I won't hear of it. I want you to go with me to the movies, just tell me your name."

I looked up at him. He looked very determined. Well in the movies it's dark and it is a good show. So I tell him my name and he starts talking, asking me all kind of questions. I won't be rude so I answer and soon we're talking up a storm. I was really enjoying myself.

After the movie, at the corner, he took my arm to cross the street. I pulled back, he just looked at me.

"I want some ice cream. Don't you want some too?"

"Oh, no!" I answer as I look across the street at all the cadets there and their girls, going in and out of the ice cream parlor. "Oh, No. your friends will see me. You don't want that."

"So what if they see us."

"But they know you had a date with Jewel, when they see me, you'll get teased."

"That's alright, I don't care," and across the street we went and of course met some of his friends, which he introduced me too. They were all nice and we were soon talking and enjoying ourselves.

On the way home I was thinking about how nice he was and his friends. I wished I was more like Jewel.

"You're quiet all of a sudden," he said.

"I was just wishing I was more like Jewel. She's so pretty and always knows what to say and make people happy. Look at me, I'm..."

"I have enjoyed being with you,'" he cut in, "You're really fun to be with. And as to looking at you …"

Now I cut in. "I can't even stand up straight, Mommy is always telling me to put my shoulders back and pull my stomach in. I try but it just makes me look worst, I try, honest I do."

"Well, you just go at it all wrong. You don't push your shoulders back. All you do is take a big breath and stretch up tall, like this," and he proceeded to stretch up taller.

"Try it," and he took a deep breath to show me how. I did and it was remarkable what it did. I could feel myself straightening out.

"See, it's not hard at all. You're just as pretty as Jewel and maybe more fun to talk to. I've really enjoyed my evening."

"Really," I answered. "I've never had so my fun. I always just watched Jewel."

We were almost home. We were on that block where there were no lights or houses. He reached out for my hand again but this time he pulled me to him and tilted up my face and gave me a kiss.

"I'm leaving in the morning to go back to my ship or I'll ask for another date," he told me.

Who's There?

Jan. 12, 2012

"Good Bye Momma. We won't be late," Vicki calls back to her Momma as she goes out the door with her Father. They're going to a 4-H meeting. Generally Momma went but lately she hasn't been feeling too good. She didn't like going out of the house.

Momma turns and looks around the house, it's so empty, she'll go into the living room and watch some television but she needs a drink first. She turns to the sink and reaches up for a glass but suddenly, the hair on the back of her neck stands up and her back goes rigid. She can't even move her arm; someone is in the house and going to get her. She can't breathe or yell, she's frozen and can't more at all.

"No, I'm all alone," she tells herself. "Just take a couple deep breaths and it'll all go away. Breathe slow and easy, see now I can move. She turns around very slowly and sees that she's all alone.

Then she hears a little noise, and she spins around and around, she can't breathe again and can't seem to stop. Her stomach hurts and so does her chest, she's having a heart attack. "OH GOD OH GOD. Help me."

Momma sits down on a chair, "I've got to stop that, I'm being silly, they went to the meeting. OH, God, did I sent them to the right meeting? It was tonight wasn't it? What if I sent them to the wrong place? OH GOD. Why can't I remember and keep things straight anymore." She ran over to the calendar, "OH Lord! I don't know which week it is, why didn't I just let them stay home."

Suddenly her hair stirs on her neck and that creepy feeling starts up her back. She spins around fast. "Who's there? Where are you? Come out so I can see you."

She sits down on the chair and begins to cry. "I've got to stop this," she takes some deep breaths and tries to calm herself. "I'm all alone and alright, I'll go into the living room and watch TV." She goes to stand up but seems froze to the chair. Come on now. Just leave loose of the seat and stand up. Take a deep breath and move.

She takes a tentative step towards the living room but she has to go past the closet. She can't seem to do that. She stretches her neck around the corner and tries to see into the living room. She can't move her feet, there she stands and can't move and can't breathe again. Her stomach is all knotted up and she's going to throw up.

The bathroom. Is someone in the bathroom? I've got to use the bathroom. OH God Help me Help me.

"Momma? We're home. Momma? Where are you?" Vicki calls as she looks around. It's just a little apartment; it only takes a second to check the bedroom and living room. Where could she be? "Momma? Momma?"

Vicki goes into the bathroom. Sees nothing and turns around but then she hears a sob. She looks again. There's Momma, jammed in a corner, down behind the commode. Her eyes are glassy and she doesn't seem to be seeing things.

"Daddy come help, Momma is in here. Something's wrong, help me."

They manage to get her out and she sees them at last.

"Momma Momma, are you alright? What's wrong?

"Momma, whatever happened? How did you get down in there?"

Momma looks around and seems to be herself again. She takes a deep breath and answers.

"Panic attack."

Christmas Gloves

"Is there any sugar for cookies, Mother?" Ernestine asks her.

"Not much but I have a recipe for a sugarless cookie I thought we would try."

"Does it have honey in? You can't eat honey."

"I know, but these will be for the little ones. We must do the best we can to make a good Christmas for them."

"Will Billy get home?"

"He's supposed to but I haven't heard. I expect he will."

It's 1936, years after the depression but the economy still isn't good. Daddy hasn't had a good steady job for a long time and it's hard making ends meet no matter how hard we try.

My big brother Billy has been sent out west to work and his money comes here, we depend on it a lot. I'm only 12 but I hear enough to know things are bad. I go and do housework for neighbors as much as I can, putting the money in the cookie jar with the rest, keeping only the pennies for myself.

Ernestine works after school too. I consider myself one of the big ones now. June is only 10 and the other three are still babies, not even in school yet. Santa has to come for them. There ought to be at least one gift for everyone. Ernestine wants some dress gloves to wear to church like the other girls. I see her looking at them at the store all the time. She knows just the ones she wants and has even tried them on. She works so hard she deserves them but they're a whole half dollar.

I'm trying to make something for everyone. Mother let me get into her scrap material so I could make June and Pruella doll dresses trimmed with bits of lace and buttons. A pillow for Ernestine but I wish I could get her the gloves. I'm saving a quarter to buy Mother some perfume and Daddy some socks. I'll never be able to save for the gloves too. I already bought the little boys whistles. I'll soon have a hankie done for Billy. It's bright red and they say they tie them around their necks in Arizonia. Now if he just gets home.

The weather is getting cold. My coat is too little, I can't button it any more but it has to do. When Ernestine put hers on to see if it would do for another winter, when she bent her arms her elbows went right through the sleeve. Mother gave her her coat, said she doesn't go out enough to have one. She stays home from church with the babies anyway. June was lucky; she got her new coat last year.

"Ernestine! What are you doing? Snooping around in Mother's closet?"

"Well, I saw Mother put some things up here and the one package looked just like the gloves I want."

"Don't look! You'll spoil your Christmas."

"No I won't, I know there's no Santa Claus. I just have to know if she got them for me. They're not at the store any more, someone bought them. I'll die if I think someone else has them."

"Please Ernestine, wait."

"Look, it is them, it is. IT IS! Now I know everything will be alright. It's going to be a wonderful Christmas.

I thought so too. Now I could get Mother the perfume and Daddy his socks. I wanted Ernestine to have those gloves too.

The days now just flew. The sugarless cookies were good. We decorated up the house with things we made; the tree was up on a table out of the way of the little ones.

A farmer friend gave Daddy a big pumpkin, another gave him some apples, they were spotted or something so that they couldn't be sold. They sure tasted good anyway. We can expect some candy and an orange from church; they always give the children that. If we wait till the last minute, Daddy thinks he can get a nice chicken at the butchers, one that hadn't sold. It's going to be a good Christmas.

Wonderful! Wonderful wasn't the word; we hadn't counted on our friends and neighbors. A knock on the door Christmas Eve was a basket of food. It even had a turkey in it. We never has a turkey before. Cookies with sugar! Sugar sprinkled all over the tops of some. Billy arrived about the same time. Now everything was perfect.

On Christmas morning when we came down stairs, we couldn't believe what we saw. Toys for the little ones. A kiddy car and small rocking horse. A doll with hair you could comb. A dump truck that the back went up, a ball and set of jacks. A Rag doll for Pruella. The neighbors had worked hard to help us have a good Christmas.

As the packages were opened, everyone 'Ooh'd and Aah'd' over everything. Mother had made new underclothes, Ernestine had made hankies. Things that we needed. There was a big box with my name on it. When I opened it, there was a coat with a fur collar. It wasn't brand new, you could tell it was used but I didn't care, it was beautiful.

"Is that all the packages?" Ernestine asks. I look up and see Ernestine holding homemade underwear, looking at Mother, where were the gloves?

"Yes, I think so." Mother answered looking around. "Is something missing?" Ernestine didn't have time to answer for right then Grandma and Grandpa came in. They had little bags of candy for everyone.

As the candy was being given out, Mother went to the buffet, opened a drawer and took out two boxes, one for Grandma and one for Grandpa. As soon as I saw that box, I knew, I looked at Ernestine and saw her face, tears came into her eyes and she turned and ran up the stairs. I went after her, she sure needed comfort now.

After a bit we went back down and helped Mother with dinner and all.

As Grandma was leaving, she turned to Ernestine, "With new gloves, I don't need these," and she handed her the old ones. Ernestine wore them proudly. Did she learn not to snoop? Of course not!

KARYLYNN RYAN

Karylynn comes from Northampton, MA and moved to Florida full time in 2010. Despite physical challenges she enjoys a happy life with her father, a retired firefighter and has dozens of friends and activities to keep her busy.

An interview with Karylynn Ryan on the subject: *"What contribution does writing make to your happiness and well being?"*

January 24, 2008

When I arrived at #657 Selkirk on Tuesday morning, there was great excitement due to the arrival of a gang of cement workers and two massive mixer trucks. A new driveway was going in across the street at Brenda and Werner's. I sat with Miss K on the porch and tried to get her to concentrate on the subject of the day. It rapidly became obvious that this was NOT the assigned topic. Ed joined us and told of the exploits of the handsome young Hispanic who was the crew boss and how he had been able to smash huge chunks of concrete with a sledgehammer and little effort. We all admired his rippling muscles and glossy ponytail.

After about ten minutes of not so silent contemplation, I again attempted to turn the conversation to writing. Ed mentioned that John had asked him why he didn't join the group but Ed said even if he wrote a piece, he'd never be able to read it back later. I refrained from asking if this was due to shyness or reluctance to share. Ed has some great stories about his life in the fire hall, as a teenager during the rock and roll era, and as a disgruntled recipient of health care in the modern age. I wish we could get him to join us; he is a great raconteur, and like Miss K, has a succinct way of making his point. Still, this piece is about what the act of writing does for us. My mind drifted a little as I watched the workmen across the street and I began to wonder, is it the writing –

the physical act – that is important, or being able to communicate your thoughts and have them evaluated by others? For Ed and his daughter I believe it is the joy of connecting with friends, neighbors and co-workers. The means of connection is really not that important after all.

Karylynn looked at me and said, **"I like when people help me with my work."** I smiled back at her and nodded. She looked at me rather pointedly. **"Write it down,"** she said. I complied.

A few minutes later she said, **"I like to talk in class about the different stories."** She smiled slowly and looked thoughtful. "It is nice to find thing out in the books and **stories people talk about."** She looked down at her notebook of work from the Phantom Stallion book. There are only a few pages left until the end of the story. We have both learned a lot from that book… about human nature, and evil, and kindness and courage and enjoyment of simple things. Without this writing class, we would have missed this experience.

"I like to tell how I feel and find out how you all feel. It is interesting." It is, isn't it? Sometimes each person at the table has something unique to say on an ordinary topic. Sometimes we all find ourselves in agreement. Our brains are working.

"I like when you come over, jj, and when I meet other people in class or at keyboard or work, and get to know them. It makes me happy." I nodded. **"You know, the keyboard concert is on February 28th. That is a Thursday and I know I won't be able to come to class. I will have to stretch out on my bed in the morning and rest up so I can do a good job at the concert. It is too hard to go to class that day too; too much sitting."**

"That's okay," I reminded her. "We will all understand." Miss K threw back her head and laughed. Smiling broadly she said, **"Mark my words! John Wright will tease me about it. Mark my words; he'll say something about it in class."** I grinned back at her. "I'll let you know!" I promised.

So I ask you, ladies and gentlemen, "Does this class contribute to Miss K's happiness and well being or not?"

How living in a gated community increases my sense of well-being

February 4, 2010

My father and I live here year round now. We used to spend half the year in Northampton, MA but this year we decided that the long drive back and forth is just too tiring. I am a special needs person and when I lived up North, I volunteered at two different jobs in my community.

Here in FL I do not volunteer but I have plenty to keep me busy! My Dad and I are early risers and we go off and do our shopping and errands before many people in the park are awake. That way we have the rest of the day free to enjoy all the activities here in the park.

I have a lot of friends here. People drop by to play cards or dominos with me. People help me with my writing. Some people just come to sit and chat and watch the people go by. I feel loved. Vera in the **Keyboard** is a very special person that I love. She calls me *Sweetie* and she helps me a lot. It is through her that I have learned to play different musical instruments. I play the maracas, the tambourine and the bells. I am an important part of the Maple Leaf Keyboard Club. There are two Keyboard and Choir concerts every year. I love performing!

I have other friends who have taught me to play *bocce.* It is a very exciting and I love to compete with others. I have friends who take me for long walks in my chair and we look at all the beautiful flowers and talk to neighbors along the way. Every week we can go to the Country Club for the *Happy Hour.* That's the best time to see everyone!

Christmas in the park is a very special time. There is a Christmas Eve parade with a social afterwards. On Christmas Day my Dad always has a big buffet party for our friends and they always bring me lovely presents. At Christmas, the Fire Club helps out with entertainment for the children during the Holidays. The Fire Club is a great group. They lend people hospital and other equipment when they need it and they collect aluminum to raise money to help children.

There is always a lot going on every day here. People can swim or play tennis, play horseshoes or lawn bowling or mini-golf; a lot of people play golf every single day! We have a *Strawberry Social*, a *Pancake Breakfast*, and a *Spaghetti Supper* – all of which raise money for the park. One of the best things is the annual *Merrymakers* show with hit tunes and skits from different times. There are a lot of talented people in that group. One of them is John who is also the leader here in the *Writers Group.*

This story is my contribution for a submission the writers are going to make to the Sales Office so people will be able to read about what a great place this is. I like John a lot even though, as my Dad would say, he likes to give me 'the Raspberry'. That means we tease each other. He makes me laugh!

If you are reading this, wondering if you would like to make this your home, I can tell you for sure that it is a happy place full of happy, active people. I am one of them. Come visit me…. I live on Selkirk.

LYNN PALMER, R.N.

Lynn, a long-time winter visitor to Florida's sunny climes, lives in Brooklin, Ontario with her husband, Tony. She is the proud mother and step-mother to three grown daughters and one adult son and proud grandmother to grandson Palmer. Before settling in Brooklin, Lynn resided in Toronto and London, Ontario; Lahr, Germany; Montreal and Ottawa.

She is a registered nurse and has served in that profession for over 40 years in a number of hospitals, a doctor's office and with the Victorian Order of Nurses. Lynn was also a senior manager with Visiting Homemakers Association, Ottawa.

Lynn was first introduced to the fun of life writing at Maple Leaf in 2009. Returning to the pleasures of an Ontario spring she pursued her passion as a member of the Whitby Seniors Life Writing group. In 2010 she was pleased to accept an invitation to facilitate a series of Life Writing courses in the newly-opened Brooklin Community Centre and Library, an endeavour that continues today.

Warriors Day

Late summer growing up in Toronto, always meant the CNE and in our house, it always meant the Warriors Day Parade.

My grandfather had been in World War 1 and was a member of the Legion, actually the President of his legion.

My grandfather was a very quiet man, but for parade day, he would put on his Legion jacket, beret and a large group of medals. He would take the event very seriously as he did November 11th, which in my day was a school holiday.

There was always solemnity around these events because my Aunt, who lived with us in my early years, had lost her husband at the Battle of Ypres. I remember asking my grandmother if Aunt had ever married and she whispered that she had and her husband had died in the War. Grandpa would do the parade and we would watch from the midway, as the soldiers marched passed from the Princess Gate to the Dufferin Gate. There were lots of military members then of both wars and the parade was long. My uncles and father who were in World WAR II, never participated in this event. My recollection was always of solemnity and often not seeing much of the parade for I was a child and little. As the years went by Grandpa faithfully did the parade, and if possible, I would see him and sometimes not.

Years pass and everyone ages, or should I say at that time, I was in my early twenties and thinking I had all the time in the world.

I didn't see my grandparents as much, being busy with my life. For whatever reason and that I can't remember, I was at the EX on WARRIORS Day, but not for any particular event. Actually, I think I forgot about the parade happening on that day.

I was near the Princess Gate, when I heard the bagpipes and band start up, they were coming from the Armoury, near the EX, at Old Fort York. There were the soldiers coming along and there in the front row was grandpa and possibly only at the most, about twenty World War I Vets, most of them were gone by now. There was my grandfather looking old, but marching to the beat of the band. He looked proud and he didn't even know I was there. I have always remembered this so well.

For that day, my heart was full of love for this old man, who lived a good life, did his duty to his country and always held in high esteem the honour and price of freedom, and who never forgot to remember such a horrible war.

The End of the Light

When I was a little girl, I lived in a house full of adults.

My Aunt Shirley would do her ironing listening to the soaps on the radio. I remember the sound of the organ playing those deep chords and actually being a little frightened of their sound, it was so mournful. I remember being absolutely upset by the drama of those people, who would cry on the radio, yell, laugh and best of all, slam doors. Did we know them, who were these people? I guess I was told it was a story and all would be alright.

In the late sixties, I picked up on this soap, which was now on TV, and called THE GUIDING LIGHT. This was forty years ago and I have been an ardent fan since then. Listening to the daily drama of life unfolding of the Bauers, the Lewises, and the Spaudlings along with other characters who would die, come back, be cloned and of course the long lost given up at birth, children's return.

It was my sanctuary at 3 pm on weekdays, if I was home and not working or busy. I even had our children hooked a bit in their teen years. I even lived abroad for 7 years and returned to the Light. We would go away, and I could watch the story anywhere we travelled in Canada and the United States. It was a safe haven from my world and as I aged, some of the story lines were not too farfetched.

For many years, no one I knew would admit this weakness of watching the soaps, but now as so many soaps like the 'Young and The Restless' are popular, it is de rigueur. Since the beginning a few years ago of reality TV, I have found the Light even more real, as the reality shows, in my mind are drivel.

Since the announcement in June that the Light would be off the air in mid September, I have been even more nostalgic.

They will be off September 18, so as it is the 16th, wanted to write this down. The characters are seemingly having happy endings, all the angst and upsets are past and there is no good or evil. Messages are given out to all to live each day with joy. Time is awasting and we should seize each opportunity we are given to enrich our lives and make the world a better place.

I like the ways my TV family has ended its long run. It had been on radio and TV for 70 years, what an honour and a life, it has enjoyed.

Goodbye Guiding Light and now as the end has come and gone, I miss you.

Wish life was like the soaps with always a very happy ending.

A Dream

It was September 8, 2001 and we were off to our nephew David's wedding in Hudson, Quebec. A perfect idyllic late summer day with bright sun, no humidity and best of all, no bugs. The wedding was lovely, followed by a reception at the Golf and Country Club. Our accommodation was at "Le Seignior Hotel" on the west side of Montreal.

We got back to our lovely room at about midnight and I fell into a deep sleep, which in itself is unusual for me. When I awoke in the morning, I was very disturbed by a most unusual dream that I had.

The dream goes like this. I am on an island and it does not feel safe. It seemed like there were no places to hide and be inconspicuous. I was wandering about, when I heard planes overhead and I was trying to hide. The planes reminded me of World War 2 bombers. The day was sunny and bright and the ground was covered in tumbleweed, not trees to hide under or behind. There was a person beside  me and I said "Come, we must try to hide," and he said to me, "Don't worry, they won't hurt us, we are Americans." With that, the plane above started shooting and I woke up in a start.

The dream bothered me and at breakfast, I remember telling family members about it and I concluded at the time that it was related to the fact that our family is half American and half Canadian, that this happened.

The day of September the 9th was another gorgeous day, but all day I had a most unsettling feeling. We did some touring of the antique stores and flea market in Hudson and I still could not shake this feeling. We headed back to Ottawa in the early afternoon and as the day turned into evening, my regular world and duties took over.

The dream safely went into the place in the brain where dreams go and can be retrieved when necessary. Monday was another lovely day and Tony went off to Toronto for a seminar. I did not work Mondays, so I enjoyed piddling about and keeping busy.

When I awoke on Tuesday, the day was another glorious one; I headed out as usual at 8:30 to take Bandit, our dog, for his romp

in the park. I came home to a ringing phone and ran to get it.

It was Mary from work, "Turn on the TV," she says. "Why?" I asked.

"Just turn it on," she says again. "Why?" I say again. And then she tells me, a plane had hit the Tower in New York, and seconds ago, another one had hit.

It was September 11, 2001.

LARRY COGLAN

Larry spends summers in rural Iowa with his wife of 44 years, enjoying horseback riding, hobby farming, antique tractors, and family. Winters are spent in southwest Florida kayaking, cycling, writing, and enjoying the balmy climate.

18 February 2009

The Adventures of Commander John Carter

CHAPTER 1

It was getting late and darkness brought dangers, more dangers than during the light of day. Commander John Carter and his two field officers, Captain Duane Daniels and Lieutenant Byron Marcus, were returning from a reconnaissance mission on the larger of two moons in orbit around the planet Zahron. Gone many years from their birth home on Earth, they were headed toward Fort Ainsworth, a lonely and fortified outpost where there was safety from the jungle creatures that thrived on this moon called Multip. Daylight on Multip lasted over 30 hours and they had been gone for most of it. They had succeeded in locating a defensible position for the next outpost in a chain of outposts for the mining consortium for whom they were employed. Their only defence, apart from their heavy and high-powered rifles, a grenade launcher, and a longsword each, was their tigerhorse, a huge beast in the early stages of domestication that served more as a guard than it did transportation. There had been stories of men attempting to ride a tigerhorse, but none with a happy ending. For a predator that weighed in excess of a ton, it could move through the jungle with astonishingly little noise.

At the bank of a large unnamed river, Attila, the name Commander Carter had given their tigerhorse, abruptly stopped.

Not unusual, given the animal's distaste of water or mud, but a low rumble from deep in Attila's throat gave the signal to drop to the ground, out of sight. Something was near, and most things on Multip found humans quite suitable as food. As Carter lay on his stomach intently searching the water, he automatically clicked the safety of his rifle to the off position. Daniels, on his stomach, watched their rear, while Marcus, on his back, searched the treetops for movement. The lips were pulled back on Attila's mouth, exposing long, curving yellow fangs over 8 inches in length. The deep rumble in his throat intensified.

"Snake," whispered Carter, "a big one crossing the river toward us, keep down." A "big one" on Multip meant a snake capable of swallowing a full-grown man, whole, with very little effort. Part way across the river, the snake had caught their scent. Its long forked tongue, the size of a man's arm, flicked the hot steamy air as it slowly lifted its head from the water to a height of 15 feet or more. Attila lowered his head, ears pinned back tight, razor sharp claws extended to their max, ready to lunge. At the first hint of a charge from Attila, the snake, whose total length was probably 40 feet or more, was capable of rising at least another 5 feet and attacking from above.

"John," said Duane from the rear, "that snake is poisonous, very poisonous. Don't let Attila fight with it, he might lose." John centered the cross hairs of his rifle between the snake's eyes and pulled the trigger. The roar of the big gun reverberated through the jungle canopy as the huge snake went into convulsions, twisting itself almost into a knot as it tried to overcome the damage of the heavy slug that had torn through its head. It thrashed and churned for several minutes before it gave up and allowed the river's current to have its way. As it floated away, John thought to himself, it will be something else's meal in a very short time.

The three men remained on the ground for a few more minutes catching their breath. The 110 degree heat and 100 percent humidity of this place had a way of draining even the most fit of soldiers. The heavy atmosphere was a near constant on

Multip and everyday downpours ensured that the jungle dripped rain all the time, night and day. Being soaked and muddy came with the job.

Byron had crawled forward on his stomach to the others. "We're gonna have to get the hell out of here, soon," he said, "that rifle blast was more than likely heard by the apemen."

CHAPTER 2

The apemen of Multip were a backward and vicious bunch having the head and teeth of a baboon like creature from earth and standing erect like an 8 foot tall human. In spite of the fact they were armed only with primitive weapons, they had the advantage of incredible strength, as well as great numbers. One could carry just so many bullets, so it was far better to avoid them if at all possible. They offered no threat to the fortified outposts, but could be a real problem to anyone caught out in the jungle. Once an outpost was finished, a wide road would be built to the next site using a combination bulldozer and battle tank. It was hoped that once the local fauna had tested the battle tank enough times, they would learn to leave it alone. This would free up soldiers for other duty. Commander Carter and his officers, however, had no such luxury as a heavily armed tank on the last leg of their expedition; they were on foot and still had several hours of travel before they would be safely back inside Fort Ainsworth.

The three men had taken temporary shelter under a huge leaf. It was big enough to keep them and their gear somewhat out of a recent and heavy downpour, the remnants of which were still dripping through the dense foliage giving the wet, spongy ground the musky smell of rotting vegetation. No one wanted to be discovered by a band of apemen, but the incessant thrum of countless millions of insects, and the constant drip of heavy raindrops would prevent their being heard if they were to approach from the rear.

Commander Carter signaled it was time to push on. There were still several hours of twilight left in the day before Multip passed behind Zahron into the darkness. Multip's twin moon, Bouch, would offer a brief, but huge, full, and very bright moon for another hour or so, before it became totally ink black. Their lives depended on being inside Fort Ainsworth before that happened.

The three men got to their feet, replaced the cold pacs inside their vests to keep their core temperature out of the danger zone, drank deeply from their canteens and moved on. They headed upstream along the bank of the river. Attila fell silently in behind.

"We need to go upstream to where the fallen tree crosses the river," said Carter.

"How much out of our way will that take us?" asked Lieutenant Marcus.

"Not sure, but it's too dangerous to cross here, too deep, and too many of them damn crocodile lookin' things under the surface," replied Carter, "I'd like to spend tonight in my own bed with the A/C cranked up to the max, and not in the belly o' one o' them foul beasts."

"Amen to that," added Captain Daniels.

The three men walked shoulder to shoulder through an area with such a heavy canopy it nearly blocked out all light. Attila's head was directly above their own, his forward looking eyes taking in everything. Shadows now gone in the increasing gloom, they marched on toward the tree that would serve them as a bridge.

"Rat-dogs to our rear," cried Lieutenant Marcus, "lets pick up the pace a bit." A small pack of the beasts posed no problem, but a large pack could be trouble. The long legged animals were a collie-sized rodent with razor sharp incisors and an insatiable hunger for flesh. Byron and Duane both pulled their long swords from their scabbards. Carter slung his rifle on his back and cradling the grenade launcher, readied it for use.

"Tree-bridge in sight," said Carter, "about 100 yards ahead. If we can make it to the bridge, we can turn them back, no matter how many there are." Carter dropped to the rear, and spinning around, took a quick estimate of their number. "Shit," he said, "I don't like this one bit." He fired a grenade into their midst sending dirt, vegetation, pieces of rat dogs and debris flying through the air.

"Only another ten yards," yelled Duane. Attila abruptly stopped in his tracks, head down and issuing a deep rumbling growl as a warning to take cover. On the opposite side of the tree bridge stood a large gathering of apemen armed with spears and clubs.

CHAPTER 3

The three men formed a circle, backs together, rifles and longswords at the ready. Attila, fangs bared, took a protective stance over them.

"OK Commander," said Captain Daniels, "what's your plan for getting us the hell outta here?"

"All right, don't panic," replied Carter, "we've been in a lot worse spots than this. Let's stick tight together and slowly move down Attila's left flank to his rear. The only way home is across that tree bridge, or swim the river, and I'm sure's hell not keen on that."

Several of the rat dogs had approached closer to Attila. He lunged out toward them, catching one with a sidelong swipe, claws fully extended. The rat dog went flying through the air, off to the side, trailing some of its entrails. It landed on its side, kicking its back feet as though trying to run from its pain. In response a half dozen other rat dogs broke from the pack and turned on their injured pack mate, ripping chunks of flesh from its still alive and howling carcass.

The three men, brandishing their longswords and rifles, slowly moved along Attila's left flank, as the rat dogs split into two packs to try to surround them and cut them off from the tree bridge. Only 10 yards lay between them and the well traveled path leading up to the massive fallen tree. Carter readied the grenade launcher.

"When I say 'when', you two take Attila onto the tree bridge about 30 feet or so," said Carter, "then stop, draw a bead on the apemen, and wait for me."

"Yes sir," said Daniels and Marcus in unison.

"GO!" yelled Carter and stepped out in front of Attila, leveling the grenade launcher at the pack of rat dogs. He lobbed a grenade into the center of their approaching front, then one to their left flank, and immediately one to their right flank. The explosions echoed through the jungle and Carter took advantage of the smoke filled mayhem to make a dash for the tree bridge. Spinning around, he crashed into Attila, who had refused to follow in the confusion of their sudden separation. Once all three men were regrouped on the tree bridge, Attila rejoined them.

"OK," said John Carter, "so far, so good." Both officers starred at John wondering where the *good* was in being caught on a fallen tree, one end of which was guarded by apemen with spears, the other end surrounded by a large pack of vicious, hungry rat dogs, not to mention the waning light of day.

The men sat on the wide trunk of the tree, rifles leveled at both ends of the bridge. Taking a few minutes to catch their breath, they replaced their cold packs again, drank another canteen full of water and waited for Commander Carter to come up with a plan that would get them safely back to Fort Ainsworth before total darkness set in.

The apemen were searching for signs of weakness and had climbed into some of the branches of the gigantic tree trying to gain a better position. The old fallen tree had clung to life and had grown a new crown in the last half century, making that end harder to defend. The rat dogs were gathered at the base end, waiting for their chance to attack.

"We're going to have to make this a full on assault." said Carter, "This is no place for defence, we're just too badly outnumbered. Lieutenant Marcus, when I give the command, shoot a dozen or so rat dogs, then turn toward the apemen and follow us, don't look back, take out as many of the apemen as you can while you run.

Captain Daniels, I want you to take out as many apemen as you can, concentrate on the ones overhead in the tree branches."

Commander Carter shouldered his grenade launcher, took aim at the left flank of the apemen on the far bank. "Ready?"

CHAPTER 4

Commander Carter pulled the trigger on the grenade launcher, sending a fragmentation bomb into the left flank of the apemen. Lieutenant Marcus fired round after round into the rat dogs, sending them scattering. The rat dogs seemed to learn faster than the apemen, who seemed oblivious to the fact that they were being killed. Captain Daniels shot one apeman after the other out of the tree branches overhead. Another grenade was launched into the left flank, followed by another. The three men started forward. A wooden spear struck Attila's tough leathery hide and bounced off. A grenade was launched into the crown of the tree, sending down bodies and tree branches all around. Another grenade exploded into the right flank, and another into the left flank. Slowly, the apemen moved to the right and the three men moved forward faster. An apeman dropped down out of the tree directly in the midst of the three men, nearly knocking the rifle out of Captain Daniels hands. In less than a second, Attila lunged forward. His enormous jaws loudly snapped shut on the apeman's mid section. A vicious head shake sent body parts flying. Attila bolted and swallowed what had been in his mouth.

The roar of the fragmentation bombs, along with the heavy rifle blasts had been joined in the middle of the battle by violent thunder and lightning, followed by rain hard enough to drown out all noise, even the thunder, in the deafening crescendo of rain, as if a waterfall from the heavens had been loosed upon them. The three men and their loyal defender, Attilla, crossed the tree bridge, and ran along the riverbank, upstream. Heads lowered to catch air that wasn't half water; they ran for their lives, not looking back.

They ran until a rocky outcrop offered a defendable perch on a flat stone. An overhead shelf of rock blocked the blinding rain. They collapsed on the ground, backs to the wall, rifles at the ready. Panting from the crushing humidity of the steaming, wet jungle, it was several minutes before anyone could talk. There seemed to be no one on their heels.

Commander Carter reached into his vest and pulled out a pair of binoculars and focused them on the end of the tree bridge, a quarter mile away.

"It would appear," said Carter, "that we just caught a break. The apemen and the rat dogs are in one hell of a battle with each other and seem to have lost interest in us. Let's rest up for a few minutes, change cold pacs again, and head for Fort Ainsworth. I, for one, plan on taking advantage of the 30 hour nights on this god forsaken moon, and sleep every damn one of them."

"Amen to that," said Captain Duane Daniels.

"Double amen to that," added Lieutenant Byron Marcus.

With fresh cold pacs and another canteen drained, the three men set out for their destination, only a few miles distant. The huge, bright, and full moon, Bouch, was quickly coming up and promised to light the rest of the way home, barring no surprises. Attila silently fell into step behind them. The drowning rain of just a few minutes ago had stopped as quickly as it had started. Rushing water was everywhere, making the going somewhat slow. There were plenty of opportunities for a misstep and a swim. By the time the swiftly moving moon, Bouch, was directly overhead, the jungle began to clear somewhat.

At last, they stepped into the clearing that had been bulldozed around the lonely outpost for security purposes and Fort Ainsworth came into full view.

"I'm sure there will be a lengthy debriefing session," said Carter, "before we can shower and eat, but it's sure hell good to be back."

EPILOGUE

The back door to Fort Ainsworth opened and a pretty young woman in her late 20's stepped out onto the porch. Cut-off jeans and a form fitting tank top, red hair in pigtails, she was truly a sight for sore eyes. Attila climbed up the porch steps, took a few laps from her water bowl and flopped down on the porch, tongue hanging out in a pant.

"What have you three been doing all day," she said, "I thought you were going to mow the yard and wash the car today?"

"Uuuuh, weelll." said Commander Carter.

"And what have you kids been doing, you promised to weed the garden while your dad mowed the yard?"

Captain Duane Daniels and Lieutenant Byron Marcus both looked at the ground, offering no comment.

"Sometimes I wonder about you guys," she said, with a shake of her head, "it's amazing how far you'll go, just to get out of doing a little work. Well, get washed up for supper, it's almost ready, and after you eat, you can give that fool dog a bath, I can't imagine how she got so muddy."

March 24, 2011

CHARACTERS

Commander John Carter. . . . . Larry Coglan

Captain Duane Daniels . . . . Dan Coglan (son, age 11)

Lieutenant Byron Marcus . . . . .Mark Coglan (son, age 8)

Young woman. . . . . Carol Coglan (wife and soul mate)

Attila . . . . Peewee (the dog)

circa 1976, Rural Route 1, Ainsworth, Iowa

BOB BITZ

Bob has found a hidden part of himself since joining the Maple Leaf Creative Writing Group a few years ago. Since then he has written and published five books dealing with agriculture and history. Previously he had owned an integrated turkey farm near Syracuse, NY.

Beware, Governments' Generosity May Destroy Us!

3/29/10

The prosperity that the people of the United States enjoy today is the result of the efforts of untold millions of Americans attempting to improve their standard of living during the past 236 years. The great majority of Americans have worked hard and created a standard of living that is the envy of most of the rest of the world. Hundreds of thousands of new businesses have been formed, providing jobs and raising our standard of living, benefiting both our country and its citizens.

As our country developed, almost all of our citizens gratefully accepted the responsibility for their own and their family's needs. They felt that government should only provide services beyond the scope of the individual, such services as law and order, fire protection, parks and formalized education. During this past century, however, we have seen a gradual increase in the role of our governments, a role that has been rapidly accelerating in both size and scope.

This large and rapid increase of the role of government, in our lives, is of grave concern to me and should also be a concern to every American. New technology and increased population require a greater role by government, but when money or goods are provided directly to our people, without effort on their part, there is a tendency for the recipient to rely on government, rather than himself, to provide for his present and future needs.

An additional concern is that millions of Americans are receiving benefits from government through programs that are unfunded or under-funded, such as Social Security, Medicare, Pensions, Medicaid and numerous other smaller programs. Unemployment benefits are extended, partial mortgage balances forgiven and credits are given to homebuyers.

Government programs, designed by government to help people, often seem warm and fuzzy at the time they are initiated. We all like to help others. Very often the short-term benefits pale in comparison to the long-term damage done that destroys the initiative of our citizens and puts our country deeply in debt.

These unfunded and under-funded public programs are insidiously eating away at the future standard of living, which our children and grandchildren might otherwise have enjoyed. The onerous debt created, weakens our country and limits its capacity as a beacon of democracy in the world. The debt created at both the State and Federal level must eventually be paid. There are only two ways to accomplish this: increased taxes and inflation, both of which are detrimental to our standard of living and to the strength of our country.

Millions of Americans are losing the incentive to improve their opportunities because of excessive government intervention in their lives. This not only is damaging to the individual, but it is also harmful to our country. In order for people to receive, without expending effort, others who are successful, must pay increased taxes to support those benefiting from government's generosity. When taxes become excessive, the incentive for the successful to create jobs decreases, resulting in fewer jobs and the entire country is the loser.

Gifts from government destroy an individual's opportunity to improve his own standard of living. Such a situation is unfortunate, but when it happens to a large portion of the population of an entire country, it is catastrophic! Beware, something for nothing may reap disastrous consequences for our country and its people.

Parting is Such Sweet Sorrow

It pains me to leave my mistress of the South. She is sweet, warm and cuddly. She holds me to her bosom, stroking my hair with a gentle hand as I glory in the softness of her touch.

Unfortunately she has another side, as most mistresses do. She can be moody, dark and even dull, sometimes turning to violent expression, making me quake with a mixture of anticipation and fear. The sudden explosions of her character, at times, bring the beauty of fireworks changing slowly from brilliant light to a subtle lingering glow. At other times she reminds me of the violent lightning flash with its ear splitting crash of thunder that sends shivers down my spine.

The time has come, but how can I leave her, this one that offers more than is anticipated, often more than is desired; this one who brings me to ecstasy and leaves me in wonderment?

However, my heart receives a call. It is from an old love, one who has never forsaken me. She is my mistress of the North. She has missed me. I know, because she always welcomes me unabashedly, seemingly knowing I will return to her.

She, like my mistress of the South has two sides, but with more subtle differences, requiring me to sharpen my senses lest I mistake her real feelings. I have seen her appear to be on the verge of a violent act, but turn away and then slowly turning back, she comes to me, with a warm, sweet, smile giving me her all. Oh what rapture to be with her, what joy she brings to my heart.

Each time I leave, one for the other, I am torn; should I leave or should I stay? Each occasion brings both sadness and anticipation of joy. I am but a pawn in the hands of each, bouncing from one to the other, and destined, again, to experience the "sweet sorrow" of parting.

How Long Shall I Love Thee?

It is the spring of adult life. Our hormones are flowing, no, not flowing, gushing! Every member, well almost every member of the opposite sex attracts, like the nectar of the flower to a bee. Then a chance meeting, perhaps it was a planned meeting; words, smiles and a date!

Oh! He/she is perfect, exactly what I have been looking for! More dates, talk, smiles and more. I can't live without you! Yes, you are my ideal, the only one for me. I love you!

Our road takes us to the summer of life and with it reality! Amazingly, perfection has disappeared. Some new verbal expressions of changing minds are interspersed with the old endearing comments:

"You don't love me anymore!"

"You'll put us in the poorhouse!"

"Can't you make the children mind just once?"

"You never pick anything up from the floor!"

The couple has come to another intersection in the roads of life. Shall we continue on the same road or each take a different path? Which road will bring the fewest obstacles, the greatest joy, and fewest headaches?

Perhaps the couple survives into the fall of life, the children have gone off to college and they come to more intersections in the road of life. There might be a new career, a significant move, additional education, or the perception, real or imagined, that the partner has changed. Which road shall I take?

There are couples that decide to diverge at one of the many intersections along the way while others follow the same highway together, living happily ever after, and still others following the same highway, fighting ever after.

What is responsible for the various differences in outcome? Research with magnetic imaging of the brains of married couples, shows there is an area of the brain that lights up when the subject, who is deeply in love with the spouse, is shown a picture of the spouse, even after many years of marriage. Why is this? Is it genetic or is it similar to putting the right ingredients together, forming a culinary delight?

Perhaps, in the future, science will be able to forecast the potential success of an anticipated marriage by examining the couple's genes, brain waves or hormones. Maybe we'll even be able to go to the pharmacy and purchase a love drug! Personally I still favor the old fashioned way. I think it's more fun to let my brainwaves and hormones do their job!

SUE DWYER

*I am originally from England, but now call Newcastle, Ontario, Canada,
my home. I have worked as an educational assistant and an elementary
school secretary. I have also taught at international schools in
Switzerland, Turkmenistan, China and Armenia. My husband and I have
4 daughters between us and 3 grandchildren.*

It's Good to be Back

December 2, 1010

The old woman heaved herself out of bed. Sharp pains jabbed
at her legs and back. She found her slippers and quietly
shuffled out of the bedroom, shutting the door softly so as not to
wake the old man still cocooned on his side of the bed.

"Funny he's not up yet," she thought, "He's always up at the
crack of dawn peeing." She went into the bathroom and gingerly
lifted up her nightdress, then carefully lowered her bottom onto
the cold toilet seat.

"Guess it's me peeing at the crack of dawn today." She laughed
softly to herself and looked around the bathroom.

"I need to paint in here," she thought, looking at the outdated
flowered wallpaper. "It must be 15 years since we did this." She
noticed some cracks in the wall and what looked suspiciously like
urine stains on the floor. She got herself off the seat, flushed the
toilet, washed and dried her hands and hobbled out to the kitchen.
An hour later she was still sitting at the kitchen table; her oatmeal
was eaten, her coffee cold, and the Sudoku and crossword were
finished.

"Strange the old fart hasn't got up yet," she thought. "Maybe
he's dead." This idea didn't seem to bother her and she stayed in

her yellow plastic chair looking out at the lake. She wasn't sure she was happy to be back in Florida.

The old man hoisted himself out of bed reluctantly. He still felt tired but he had to pee urgently. He moved as quickly as he could towards the bathroom sans slippers. He made it just in time, although several drops didn't quite hit the target. He looked around the bathroom.

"I love this room," he thought, "It always makes me smile early in the morning with its yellow and blue flowers, so bright and cheery." He remembered wallpapering it as a surprise for the old bat, in the days when he gave a damn. She had been very appreciative! Forgetting to flush the toilet and wash his hands, the old man shuffled down the hall to the kitchen. He stopped and stared, momentarily confused by the scene before him. The old woman was sitting at the table with her face in a bowl.

"What the Sam hell are you doing, you stupid old bat?" he cried. When she didn't respond, he turned away, poured himself some coffee, put on his favourite hat and went out onto the back porch. Sitting in his rocker he looked out at the lake.

"Maybe she's dead," he thought. The idea didn't seem to bother him.

"It's good to be back!"

Dancing in the Rain

"What a deluge!" remarked the wrinkled faced old lady, as she shook her umbrella and shuffled her large body into the bus shelter.

"It's perfect weather for ducks!" replied the elderly gentleman sitting erect on a small bench.

"May I sit next to you?" asked the woman politely.

"Be my guest!" replied the main, smiling and shifting over slightly to his right. He looked at his new companion and noticed her grey hair had been recently permed. Her lips were stained with a deep shade of red.

"Do you have far to go?" he asked.

"Oh, I'm not getting the bus," she said. She opened her purse and took out a mirror. Inspecting her face, she licked a finger and tried to wipe off some mascara that had smudged under her eyes.

"Do you live around here?" asked the man.

"No, not exactly," she answered. She returned the mirror to her purse.

"I'm going to visit my daughter," explained the man, "She lives near the Exhibition in Toronto." The woman made no comment. She put her umbrella and purse on the ground. She began unbuttoning her wet coat.

"Is it hot in here, or is it me?" she inquired. The woman struggled out of her raincoat and dropped it on the ground.

"I think it must be you!" laughed the man, nervously. To his horror, the woman then took off her white blouse and sat calmly in her lace bra and long black skirt.

"That's better," she said and smiled sweetly at him, showing small uneven yellow teeth.

"The rain seems to be getting worse," said the man trying to behave as if nothing strange was happening. The woman stood up and unzipped her skirt, letting it drop to the ground. As she had no underwear on, this caused the man to become quite alarmed.

"Really, madam, I think you should put some clothes on!" he exclaimed. The woman ignored him. The man wished the bus would arrive and he could escape from the mad woman sharing his bench.

"They are watching me, you know," whispered the woman.

"Who is watching you?" replied the man, becoming more confused.

"Them." The woman inclined her head towards the corner of the shelter. The man looked but saw only some old bus transfers stuck to the wet floor and a few cigarette ends.

"They want me to dance, but I hate dancing," she explained.

"I see," said the man. He stood up.

"I think the bus is coming," he said as he made his way to the door.

"Don't let your daughter dance, will you?" asked the nearly naked woman.

"No, of course not," answered the man as he hurriedly stepped out into the rain. To his relief, the bus drew up against the kerb and the doors whooshed open. The man climbed onto the bus and showed the driver his transfer. He found a seat and looked out of the window at the shelter. As the bus pulled away he saw a large naked woman dancing in the rain.

Insatiable Curiosity

The lion sank her large canines into the neck of her prey, cutting off its life giving breath. She had stalked the young gazelle, which had become separated from her mother, and then chased her down in a violent scramble for survival; the lion starving for food, and the gazelle desperate for escape and life.

The lion and her cub had covered many miles over the past week, searching for food and water. The waterholes were almost dry. Surviving the worst drought in five years would be a miracle. Her cub bounded over to the kill and began tearing at flesh; hunger overcoming any other emotion. The lion was exhausted. Killing had taken all her strength. Even eating was difficult. She let her cub eat its fill. Later, she slept; a sleep so deep she did not hear her cub move away from her side.

It wasn't hunger that moved him this time, just his insatiable curiosity. What was that? There was a rustling in the bush and a flash of color. He crept towards the low lying scrub. Another noise, like the cry of a wounded animal, carried on the wind towards the cub. Sniffing the air, he detected a strange odour, certainly not an animal smell he knew. He batted the bush with his large paw. The small animal was lying on its back, its arms and legs were jerking violently back and forth, and a wailing sound came out of its mouth. The cub moved slowly closer and sniffed the strange creature. It was a foul smell of feces, blood and something else; something unknown.

The creature became still. Its eyes locked onto the cub. Its mouth opened and an odd gurgle sounded in its throat. It kept staring at him. The cub slowly eased itself forward and brought its nose close to the alien animal. He licked the creature's hairless skin, tasting blood and salt. An arm jerked suddenly and hit the cub on the nose, startling him so much that he jumped sideways and tripped over the leg of a much bigger animal, half buried in the bush. The stench of death billowed up into his nostrils. Frightened, the cub raced quickly back to his mother. She would know what this thing was. He tried to wake her: he bit her tail, ears and muzzle, but she did not stir. Something was wrong. He called her name over and over. Finally the cub lay down by her side utterly weary. When he awoke, it was dusk. His mother felt strangely cold. The fetid stench of death arose from her body. The cub cried and pawed at her face. He didn't know what to do. Once again, he heard a noise from the bush. Reluctantly he left his mother and returned to the unknown animal. It seemed to be dying too. The cub was cold, so he lay down beside the creature and licked its face. As the night blanketed their world, two orphaned young of the African plain, a lion cub and a human child, lay side by side awaiting the dawn.

The Apple Pie

The aroma of cooked apples, cinnamon and nutmeg wafted from the kitchen, curled its way up the stairs, along the hall, under a bedroom door and into the nostrils of the child lying asleep in her bed. Her eyelids fluttered open and she breathed in the delicious bouquet. Sleep left her and she scrambled out of bed, put on her slippers and robe and hurried downstairs.

"Mummy," she called, "Are you making an apple pie?" Mummy wasn't in the kitchen, but the pie was, cooling on a rack. The girl pushed a chair to the counter and climbed up to inspect the work of art. She could see steam coming from the hole in the centre of the pie, so she knew it was still hot. The crust was brown and shiny looking. Her mouth watered. Maybe she could taste just a small piece of the crust? There were footsteps on the stairs, so the girl got off the chair quickly and pushed it back to the table. Her brother appeared.

"Where's the pie?" he asked.

"Over there," said the girl pointing. Her brother didn't need a chair; he just stood looking at the beautiful dessert and inhaled the scent of the apples and spices.

"Where's Mum?" he asked.

"I dunno," replied his sister.

"I'm going to cut a piece!" he declared.

"You'll get in BIG trouble!" warned the girl. There were more footsteps on the stairs and a large hairy man appeared in the kitchen. His belly stuck out like a woman's pregnant stomach. He scratched it absently and sniffed.

"Hey, pie!" he exclaimed, "I hope you kids weren't thinking of touching that?"

"We were just looking, Dad," said the boy. The man poured some coffee and sat at the table.

"Where's Mum?" he asked.

"I dunno," the children chorused.

"Hmm..." mumbled the man, "Well, perhaps we could have a small taste, what-der-yer-think?"

"Yes!" shrieked the kids with glee. They found plates and cutlery. Their Dad carefully cut three small pieces and they all sat around the table. The apple, pastry and spices landed in their mouths bringing an intense burst of flavour that swirled around on their tongues tasting like little pieces of heaven.

"Mmmmmmmm..." They all groaned with pleasure.

"Can we have seconds?" asked the boy.

"Good idea!" said his dad and cut three bigger slices. They gorged on the delicious apple pie. Suddenly they heard the garage door slam.

"It's Mummy!" squealed the girl.

"Quick, go back to bed!" said her dad. He dumped the plates and forks in the dishwasher. They all raced upstairs, leaving the evidence of their crime on the table: a few slices of pie and some telltale crumbs. They waited for all hell to break loose; their ears strained to hear a sound but there was nothing: no screams, yells or cursing; no stomping, smashing, no cupboards banging. The suspense was killing them, so they crept downstairs and peered into the kitchen.

Mummy was sitting at the table, her fork stabbing at the remains of the pie; her cheeks stuffed with apple and pastry and a look of rapture on her face.

Game, Set and Match

December 9, 2010

The sun made an appearance at 6:49 in the morning gracing the sky shyly with its first blush of light. The tennis court was still dark. All was quiet. A windsock fluttered gently in the breeze and a few leaves blew in fits and starts across the court becoming trapped in the net.

An empty ball machine sat waiting to be filled in the middle of the service line. At the opposite end of the court lay Charlotte Small, enveloped in an interesting mixture of blood and yellow tennis balls. She was splayed out on her back like a child making an angel in the snow. A new pink Wilson tennis racquet lay clutched in her hand in readiness for the next shot. Her white visor sat askew on her head. Charlotte's blue skirt had risen up to reveal plump white thighs, in contrast to her tanned legs, and on the right sole of her white Nike shoe was a piece of gum embedded in one of the treads.

Charlotte Small's deep blue eyes were wide open, looking quite surprised; shocked perhaps, but what stood out as most upsetting and downright unfortunate, was the tennis ball stuck in her mouth.

The sun moved higher in the sky revealing the horrific tableau to the world. Soon the ladies will be arriving on their bikes or golf carts to play, socialize and enjoy their game of tennis. There will be gasps, screams, tears and poor old Esther Mayhew will faint on top of Judith Seymore, causing more confusion and upset.

In an emergency, usually a leader emerges, ready to organize the crowd and take charge of the situation, and luckily for everyone, Miss Merry Shaw will step up to the plate, or should that be court?

"Linda, phone 911!" She will roar in her loud teacher voice. While Linda will scurry off, thankful to be away momentarily from the spectre of Charlotte's predicament, Merry will move closer to the body just to make sure Charlotte is actually dead. She is now and still will be then.

The air will explode with sirens and wails as a fire engine, ambulance and police car will scream to a halt in front of the courts. Statements will be taken. A police photographer will capture the scene on film from every conceivable angle. Yellow Police tape will be stretched across the gate cutting off access to anyone but Scene of Crime Officers. The words, "Foul Play" will be whispered by all and sundry.

None of this will matter to Charlotte Small. For her, it is, I'm afraid, already Game, Set and Match.

RALPH WOOLVERTON

Ralph has been an owner in Maple Leaf Estates (MLE) since 1979. He was born in B.C. and brought up in Winnipeg. At 17 he went to the Northwest Territories (NWT) to work with the Hudson's Bay Company as an apprentice fur-trader. He joined the Royal Canadian Air Force (RCAF) in 1942, and served as a navigation officer on the RAF Ferry Command, delivering bombers across the Atlantic and as far east as India. After the war he attended three universities and earned his PhD from McGill University in 1953 in mineral exploration and mineral economics. He is a registered Professional Engineer in the Province of Ontario. His writings tell stories from his childhood, family genealogy, animal encounters, wartime adventures, and geological field experiences.

A Child's Bedtime Story

When we moved the boys into separate bedrooms, Carol got the largest bedroom for herself. She was six years old, and she wanted the room repainted and redecorated. She chose the wallpaper that went on one wall. It was bright, colourful wallpaper showing Mexican scenes. I can see it now!

The story started a few days after the wallpaper was installed. Carol, warm and sleepy, snuggled down in bed, asked for a bedtime story: "Tell me a story about those boys on the wallpaper."

I looked at the wallpaper, and there were three little boys, repeated many times on the pattern, walking together on a sandy road with tall cactus in the background. "They are three little brothers that live in Mexico," I said.

"What are their names?" Carol asked.

I had to think fast and come up with authentic boys' names that sounded possibly Mexican, I said "They are Carlo and Pedro and Jojo."

I didn't realize the trap I was setting for myself. I continued, "The tallest boy is Carlo—he is eight years old, Pedro is the middle boy, he is six, and I think Jojo, the little guy, is about four years old."

Then more questions; after a short pause, she said, "You said they lived in Mexico. Where is Mexico?"

I answered, "Mexico is a big country many miles south of here. It is always warm and sunny there; they never get snow."
Carol looked at the pictures with sleepy eyes, and asked; "Why are Carlo and Pedro wearing shawls, and why doesn't Jojo have one?" The power of observation in small children is amazing; I hadn't noticed this difference.

Thinking fast, I said, "Those shawls are called ponchos, and are common in Mexico. Carlo and Pedro are going to school, but Jojo is too young for school, so he stays home with his mother; maybe that's why he's not wearing a poncho."

Carol asked, "Why is Jojo carrying a chicken?"

I looked at the pictures on the wallpaper carefully, and sure enough Jojo had a small white and black chicken tucked under his arm. The trap tightened. I answered, "Maybe he can't have a pet puppy or kitten, so Jojo has a pet chicken."

My daughter giggled and said "That's silly; does the chicken have a name?"

Again I had to think fast, and came up with the only Spanish word I knew: "The pet chicken's name is Pollo (*pronounced 'Poyo'*). Sometimes Jojo takes Poyo for a walk on a leash."

Carol spoke sleepily, "That's a silly story, but I love it, especially about Jojo, I love him. Thank you, Daddy." She rolled over and went to sleep.

The next night at bedtime the story was repeated. I wasn't allowed to change a single word! I was trapped into retelling the same story as it became a bedtime tradition. I told it time after time, night after night; being held exactly to the original, as she watched the three main characters on the wallpaper until she went to sleep.

After over fifty years, Carol remembers my bedtime story better than I do, and she still corrects me on even the smallest details. Last Sunday when I talked to her on the phone, and I recited this bedtime story as I wrote it, she said, "It wasn't a chicken that Jojo carried, you said it was a rooster."

My Wolf Escort

January 20, 2011

Mr. Merriweather's cabin was the last house on the bush road to the landing on the northern Ontario lake. His yard was where the snowplough turned. I parked my pickup truck in his clearing late in the March afternoon, expecting my field crew to pick me up there. "Your boys were here two days ago," said the old prospector, "but they didn't say anything about expecting you in today."

"It's only five miles down the lake to our claims; I'm not going back into town so I might as well hike to the camp. Thanks for the coffee, George, I'd better get going. It'll be dark before I get there."

Within a few minutes, I was out on the ice of the lake, with my small backpack, and rather enjoying the still frosty air of the early evening. I welcomed the prospect of an invigorating walk on the packed snowmobile trail leading to our bush camp on our uranium prospect.

Half an hour later, I caught sight of six dark shapes against the wooded shoreline, and when they raced out toward me I recognized them as a pack of timber wolves.

What should I do? Don't run! Stand still? Keep walking? I chose to keep walking, remembering that there is no record of a wolf attack on humans in Ontario. If you do get eaten by wolves how are you going to report it? The wolf pack came closer and encircled me. I kept walking. The wolves resembled very large, very gaunt dogs. They separated into a large circle about thirty feet from me; then they started to run in the circle with me in the center.

I realized hopefully that they were not going to attack me if I just continued to walk normally, and after my initial apprehension, I took a genuine interest in their behaviour.

Four wolves would run while the other two sat down. Then four would sit down while two jumped up and ran the circle around me! What a strange performance! Then all six wolves would run the circle as I kept walking. Night started to close in so I stopped and got my flashlight out of my packsack, while all six wolves sat down and waited patiently. When I resumed walking, they started to run their circle around me again, alternating sitting and running. Our strange procession continued down the lake for at least an hour as nightfall approached. The wolves left me when the lantern lights of the bush camp came into view as we rounded a rocky point. I continued on to the warm cook tent, walked in, surprised the crew and joined them as they sat at dinner.

Is it possible that the wolves were playing a game with me, and had no intention of attacking me? Maybe they sensed instinctively my family symbol or totem, and were trying to make friends, or were protecting me. Three wolves appear on the medieval family coat- of- arms. Sir Raoul de Wolfe was a Norman knight at the Battle of Hastings in 1066. He was granted land on the Isle of Wight where he founded the fortified town of Wolfe i.e. Wolfverton, hence Woolverton. His descendent, Sir Ralph de Woolverton(!), donated two trusty bowmen to Edward III's army for the defence of the realm. The little hamlet of Woolverton on the Isle of Wight disappeared when they built the island airport over it during WWII.

My friendly wolf pack on that frozen lake might have been part of the family, or possibly they thought I should join their pack.

"Doctor," I asked, "why do my canine teeth tingle, why do my ears itch, why does hair grow on the back of my hands, and why do I get a primal urge to run in the woods and howl whenever there is a full moon?"

Part of this true story appeared on the Canadian Wildlife Federation *website.*

A Fashionable Beginning

Would you believe that the formation of Canada as a nation can be traced back to a fashion trend in men's hats in Europe in the 16th century? The fashion for the beaver hat made from felt made from the under-fur of the beaver pelt lasted well into the 18th century. European quality hat makers demanded better beaver pelts than Russia could supply.

The best beaver pelts came from the northern part of North America. As early as 1634 one report says that twenty knives were traded for one prime beaver skin. The Indians thought the white man was foolish because beaver skins were so easy to come by, whereas knives were so valuable. Furs obtained by trading with the Indians became the prime export to Europe by the early 1600s. This set forth economic forces that spread the fur trade industry across the continent, and ultimately resulted in a new northern nation from sea to sea to sea, but these same forces destroyed the aboriginal culture.

Fur traders Groseilliers and his brother-in-law Radisson, reached James Bay in 1665, and returned to Quebec with reports of the fur potential of the country north of Lake Superior. They were unsuccessful in getting financial support in Quebec, Boston, or Paris, but found favorable hearing in King Charles II's court in London.

After one very lucrative venture in 1669 into Hudson Bay, the Hudson's Bay Company (HBC) Charter was drawn up on May 2, 1670. It was given monopoly over, and trading rights to all the land drained by waters flowing into Hudson Bay. This vast land area was called 'Rupert's Land' after the king's nephew who was also an investor. It was 15 times larger than the British Isles and 5 times larger than France. The Company started establishing trading posts on Hudson Bay in 1671 to trade with the Indians for fur.

The land was sold to the new Dominion of Canada in 1868 for 1.2 million dollars. This was a much better deal than the 7.2 million dollars that the U.S. paid for Alaska, and was for much more productive land, especially agricultural land.

The founding of the Northwest Company (NWC) in Montreal in 1776 was to provide direct competition with the HBC, mostly within Rupert's Land and westward to the Athabasca-Mackenzie area and beyond to the Pacific coast.

One of the founders of the Northwest Company was Alexander Mackenzie who first descended the Mackenzie River to the Arctic Ocean in 1789, and then reached the Pacific by canoe routes in 1793. He just missed Captain Cook by a few weeks there at the outlet of the Bella Coola River to the Pacific.

The relationship of the HBC and the NWC was one of trade rivalry and battles: as the trade in furs declined, both companies showed little or no profit, and in 1821 the two companies merged into the HBC.

The two companies had established and maintained British interests across the northwest part of North America for two centuries. The network of canoe routes, developed by French-Canadian *voyageurs* across Lake Superior, and westward formed the extension of a new nation, founded on July 1, 1867, with custody and promise of the second largest nation in land mass in the world.

The transcontinental railways, the establishment of the RCMP, and the granting of provincial status to Manitoba, Saskatchewan, Alberta and British Columbia, firmly established the solidarity and security of the new nation. Newfoundland joined by plebiscite in 1949 because of the attraction of Canada's social programs.

So if we examine history carefully and maybe with some creativity, we can trace Canada's origins back to men's beaver hat fashions in Europe almost 400 years ago.

March 4, 2010

My Conversation with Bear

Picture one early June morning in the Yukon mountains, a wilderness exploration camp serviced only by helicopter. I was up in the gold recovery shack on the terrace above the camp on the gold creek, making my usual early morning radio sked with the Company base in Vancouver. I heard a noise on the snow porch of the building. I thought it was one of my high school student helpers.

"Hey, Tony, would you take these boxes down to the cook? She's going out on the chopper to Whitehorse today and she asked me to bring her two or three boxes."

No answer.

"Hey! Tony?" There was still no answer.

I opened the door to talk to Tony, and came face to face with a black bear! He was as startled as I was. I slammed the door and sat down to recover from the shock of the encounter. Half an hour later I cautiously peered out the door, but the bear was not in sight. So, gathering my courage and carrying three boxes for the cook, I headed down the trail in the bright morning sunshine to get my breakfast.

Suddenly, there was the bear coming back up the trail, heading towards me! What to do? I just stood still with the three boxes in my arms. When he got closer, I said:

"Hi there, Mr. Bear!" No answer, but the bear showed no fright and came closer. So I said:

"How are you doing, Mr. Bear?" No answer, but he came even closer. So I asked him:

"How are you doing in this Yukon wilderness? Don't you get cold? Where did you den up for the winter? Where is your mate? I hope she is not around, one of you is enough!" The bear still did not answer me, and by this time he had drawn so close and so curious that he was actually in my shadow and peering up at me as I talked to him. It was almost as though he was trying to understand what I was saying. What else can you say to a wild bear that is less than three feet from you? Probably just enough to keep your own courage up. Then I said:

"Well, Mr. Bear, I think you're close enough, and I can't think of anything more to say to you, so ....Goodbye!"

With that shout I ended my one-way conversation with the bear, and flung the empty boxes at him. This startled him so much that he scrambled off into the bush, and I hastened down the trail to my camp tent keeping a close look out behind me in case he decided to follow me.

A few minutes later I heard a shriek from the kitchen. The bear had come down to the camp and had tried to get into the kitchen through an open window, obviously drawn by the smell of pancakes and bacon. The cook, a formidable woman, had attacked him with a heavy frying pan and had driven him away. The last one-way conversation the bear heard, and apparently understood, was the cook's words:

"Get the hell out of here!"

The bear fled and never came around again; he had obviously had enough of these strange one-way conversations with humans.

January 13, 2010 – A true story.

WALT LEMON

Walt was born and raised and spent most of his life in Ontario, and currently resides in Toronto and Maple Leaf in Florida He is married to Betty and they have two children (Steve (Lisa) and Janis (Glenn)) and three grandchildren (Addison, Jack and Theo). He started writing when he joined the Maple Leaf Creative Writing Group a few years ago. In 2008 he began writing his book titled "Golfing Links Courses in the British and Emerald Isles — Canadians and Their 'Annual Once-In-A-Lifetime' Trips", which was published in 2011.

The Homecoming

Her father had phoned from the farm. "You have to go meet the train, he's coming home."

She was only 25 years old, with a seven month old child, living in town, away from the farm, learning to keep a house for her husband and look after a baby.

How could she do all this and now go meet the train as well?

She did not have a car, did not know how to drive. How was she going to be able to get to the station to meet the train? She called a friend or two, but could not make contact with anyone, they were probably at work.

Should I see if one of the neighbours could drive me? Was there anyone else I could call? Brother Wilbert is away, so he can't help. What am I to do?

Is there no one else? Nope, no one comes to mind, walking with the baby buggy is my only option. It is a hot August afternoon and it's almost a mile to the station, but I can manage that!

She made sure Gordon was clean and dressed in his brightest clothes, and ensured he had a toy. He was a good baby, but he would have to endure all the waiting, the hustle and the bustle.

She hurriedly changed her own clothes, and checked to make sure that she was appropriately dressed. She wheeled the creaky old buggy with Gordon down Sproule Street to Main, then west on Main to the busiest intersection in town. *Must be careful crossing this busy road, keep Gordon safe!*

Another three-quarters of a mile in the heat!

Is that the train whistle? Is the train early? Patience, I'll get there in time. Why me? Why do I have to do this?

How could she deal with all the emotions and the solemnity of what she had to do? *Am I up to this task? I have to be strong, I am representing my family. My father needs me to do this. I can do it!*

No matter how much dread she felt, she knew how important it was that she be there.

She was hot and perspiring when she finally reached the train station; this old hand-me-down baby buggy did not roll very smoothly. She found a bench in the shade, made sure Gordon had his bottle and was ready to sleep, and sat to try to keep her emotions in check. She was not alone here now, as there were many others quietly and solemnly awaiting this train.

The whistle blew long and low as the train slowly crawled to a stop. Lots of smoke and steam! Lots of bunting draping the many rail cars!

She was here to meet her 19 year old baby brother, Corporal Wallace Wyvill, Royal Regiment, home from France, killed in action eight miles south of Caen on August 7, 1944.

January 14, 2010

Scared

I never thought that I would ever watch someone being killed, but it almost happened. I have never been as frightened in my life.

I worked for my father, a general contractor, for two summers as I was finishing high school. He had two men working for him full time, and I added an extra body to the crew. The job this summer day in 1964 was to repair a barn that was spreading. If you have ever been in one of the large barns you see throughout Ontario, you will know that they have about four levels to them, and are framed with heavy, roughly hewn Rock Elm timbers. Typically, the lowest level is the stone foundation that houses stalls for cattle, horses, pigs and other livestock. The next level is the floor of the barn itself, and it usually has a ramp leading up to double doors, where wagons full of hay, straw or grain can be driven right into the barn for off-loading. Often, you would find a granary for grain storage on this level. Stretching upwards from the floor would be at least one, and sometimes, two sets of cross timbers, which held the barn together and provided for hay storage, often to depths of 25 to 30 feet. The high roof was generally covered with sheets of galvanized steel.

This particular barn had been emptied, as the end walls were beginning to sag outwards. The beams were all sound, but some of the mortise and tenon joints needed to be replaced, after the walls were pulled back into place. Our approach was to hook a ¾ inch steel cable around both end beams, and connect them with a turn-buckle. The cable was slowly tightened by turning the turn-buckle with a heavy six-foot pry bar. This took a great deal of effort, and every one of us was sweating profusely in the hot, airless barn. We had a tremendous strain on the cable, as we had been tightening it for quite some hours, and the end walls were slowly being pulled back into position. The cable was fairly singing, it was so tight, with 20 to 30 tons of pressure on it.

My father was standing on a cross-beam, a good 20 feet off the barn floor. The rest of us were on the floor itself, struggling to tighten the turn-buckle even more. Suddenly, with a horrible screech, the turn-buckle let loose. The three of us dropped to the floor as fast as we could, as the cable went whistling across the barn like a hot knife. All I could think was that my dad would be cut in half by the flailing weapon that the cable had become. As soon as the cable stopped its thrashing and banging off the end walls of the barn, I nervously looked up to see where my dad was. He was still standing on the beam! I could scarcely believe my eyes. How had he missed being hit by that hissing, slashing cable? How had he kept his balance and not fallen?

There was no more work that day. No one had any appetite to try that cable again that quickly, and everyone was extremely jittery. My dad had a bottle of whiskey stowed somewhere in the truck, and he and his two hired men immediately had a great gulp of it. Being too young, none was offered to me. The whole scene has stayed with me to this day. I can still see and hear that cable scything and whistling through the air. We all lived and a tragedy was avoided.

December 3, 2009

Speed

We must get off the mark quickly with lots of power, get the speed up to 130 kilometres per hour, run a true line and keep resistance to a minimum. We demand Gold and nothing else.

We all have our unique responsibilities; we have trained and practised for years to develop the aptitudes and skills required for successful pursuit of this Medal. We each have our own methods, specialties and skills, but most importantly we must bring these assets together to form a cohesive team, the only way we have a chance to win.

We must be strong enough to create the speed required. Strength comes from long hours in the gyms, plus running the steep slopes and long stairs, and repetitions to create the muscle needed for the push-off.

Speed is more than strength and a strong push-off. It includes finding the correct line to your objective, starting quickly and out-racing your opponents in those first crucial seconds. One person alone with speed will not accomplish our goal, everyone must build up their speed to complement their strength.

Concentration is the third key component. If anyone is out-of-sync, failure is the only potential result. We must be 100% focused as soon as we get on the ice. We must all be ready, be attuned to the need to start strong, and keep our head in the game every second. A single lapse could ruin all our efforts.

Teamwork is absolutely mandatory. Everyone must know their position, their role, and their responsibilities for every aspect of our performance. From beginning to end, only a cohesive team can produce the success we have been training towards for four long, arduous years, and for some of us, many more years.

The moment has arrived; our event is on international TV in almost every country of the world and in front of thousands of spectators. Now is the time to reap the rewards of all the toil. It is now time to bring our strength, our speed, our concentration and our teamwork to the peak of effectiveness. We need to get off the mark with a tremendous burst of opening speed and must concentrate to keep our speed at the maximum. We must endure the frozen bumps and the g-forces from sudden turns and violent movement. We must both keep our heads up and our heads down, and must run the true line.

Thundering down a bobsled run in a four-man bob at speeds up to 130 kph, the g-forces reach as high as 5-g's on some of the turns. Your butt feels like it is dragging on the ice. Your stomach and internal organs are all pressed to the bottom of your body. The pilot must keep his head up to steer the perfect line. The rest of the crew keep their heads down to minimize wind resistance as we climb up and drop off the steep sidewalls of the track, accelerate off the long curves into 270 degree turns, and zip down the straight-away gaining ever more speed, all essential secrets to success. As we reach the finish, the whole team gasps for air that has been forced from our lungs by the g-forces.

We have won the Gold Medal! We will proudly stand on the podium at the playing of O Canada.

I have experienced part of it. I know what it feels like, as I rode the four-man bob-sled on the Olympic Track in Calgary.

What a thrill!

March 11, 2010

Passport – Mission Accomplished

"I'm sorry, sir, but you will not be flying with us tonight" stated the Air Canada check-in agent with a look that was part smile and part grimace. "Your passport has expired."

"But I have to get to Glasgow, I have made all the arrangements for 22 golfers to play all the great courses of Scotland, and I have all the paperwork. Plus it is Sunday evening of Victoria Day weekend, how can I get a new passport now?"

"Sorry, you will need to get that new passport before you can fly."

I truly wish I had been there to see the look of horror on my buddy Don's face. The annual trip to play golf in the UK was in full swing, with a few of us already having played four games and the rest arriving on a Monday afternoon. Everyone was there but the organizer, Don. Where is he? An e-mail to Perk's Blackberry said he had been detained, would arrive in a day or two. Is he okay? Did he have an accident? Was someone seriously ill? Our friend Don does not miss these trips, especially as he has all the paperwork and the payment records.

We played Dunbar Golf Club on a cool, dampish Monday afternoon, and my friend Bill Perkins took this photo of me with his Blackberry and sent it to Don with the message "Lemon hitting a shot at Dunbar, wish you were here." The return note

arrived mere minutes later stating "I will be there sooner than you think."

We did not know what was happening, but you can well imagine the surprise late the following afternoon when Don was sitting in the lounge of our hotel when we returned from golf.

"What caused your delay?" "How the hell did you get here?" "How did you get a new passport?" "How did you change your plane tickets so easily?" The questions flew in a barrage.

But Don had had almost 48 hours to prepare a defence for his embarrassing mistake, as he had recently sent a note to all of us reminding us to check our passports.

"I just told them who I was and what my emergency was. They immediately jumped to it and got me a new passport in 12 hours on a holiday. No big deal for someone of my stature."

Only later did the full story emerge. He had had to take a cab home, and decided during the ride to phone Citizenship and Immigration in Ottawa. He was able to contact someone who listened to his plight, told him he did not think much could be done, but that he would try to contact someone in the Toronto Passport Office, but not to expect much.

About 9:00 a.m. the following morning, the holiday Monday, Don received a call from the Manager of the Passport Office on Victoria Street. She stated that she needed three references, a completed set of forms with passport photos, and if he could get all of that, she would meet him in the arcade near the office at 12:00 noon. Don scrambled and got everything gathered, photos taken and signed and made it there by noon. Shortly thereafter, the Manager appeared, took his forms and a significant payment (my guess is $350 or more) and returned about 12:30 with a new passport.

Part one completed, now to tackle Aeroplan, as he was using points for his flights. He immediately called the Aeroplan office, explained his plight and discussed a variety of options for getting to Scotland. The best alternative was to fly to Frankfurt, then to Manchester, and then drive eight hours to North Berwick, just east of Edinburgh where we were staying. He immediately agreed, received the new e-tickets and headed to Toronto Pearson Airport once more.

Even in the most difficult situations, there always seems to be a way to resolve it. But just imagine, getting a new passport within 12 hours on a Holiday weekend. Impossible!

November 18, 2010

THE HONOURABLE A.C. HAMILTON

As a lawyer in Roblin, Melita and Brandon Manitoba, Al practiced civil and criminal defense law in Magistrates Courts, County Courts, the Court of Queen's Bench, Court of Appeals and, on two occasions, the Supreme Court of Canada.

He was then appointed as a Judge of the Court of Queen's Bench for the Province of Manitoba in Canada, moved to Winnipeg and presided over all manner of cases throughout the province.

After ten years in the General Division, he was appointed the Chief Justice of the Family Division and become a member of the Judicial Court of Canada. While he was on the bench he was appointed to the study 'The Aboriginal Justice Inquiry in Manitoba'. When he returned, he started a business in arbitration and mediation and wrote his first book A Feather Not A Gavel, *pertaining to the Aboriginal Study.*

Al has written two other books recounting his experiences: Country Lawyer – City Judge *was published in 2007, and* The Jailbirds *was published in 2011.*

Al is a long time participant in the Maple Leaf Creative Writing Group.

A Time of Glory?

I finally turned 18 and could join up.

The Air Force wasn't training pilots at the time so I spurned their other options and tried the Navy. If I signed up with them I could have worn their glamorous bell-bottom trousers, but would have to train as a cook. My mother hadn't taught me to boil an egg, so I declined the offer. My visit to Fort Osborne Barracks confirmed that the Army was taking all the recruits they could find.

Before I knew what had happened, I signed on the dotted line; saw a doctor who gave me a variety of shots, and a Quartermaster who gave me a khaki uniform. My arms ached from the shots, as I was herded with all my belongings to a bed for the night. I don't even remember eating.

The next day, we were taken to Minto Armouries where a Sergeant made us march for an hour. We shot 22 calibre rifles in the firing range for awhile and were then bussed to the Fort Garry campus of the University of Manitoba where the army had taken over the male and female student residences for the duration of the war.

We lined up in alphabetical order and were assigned our living quarters, three to a room. Next, our whole company was lined up in the hall, stark naked, for a "short arm inspection" by a doctor. The hooting and hollering by some of the tough guys was unnerving.

Those two or three months at the University seemed committed to exhausting us. We had to run everywhere we went, unless we were learning how to march in quick time or how to put on a gas mask in a hurry. Our Sergeant had had fighting experience in Italy and was tough. One of his favourite exercises was to have us crawl across a field without being seen.

On one of the coldest days of one of the coldest winters in history, we were taken by train to Shilo for advanced training with live ammunition. By the time we ran the three miles uphill from the station to our "H-Hut" carrying all our belongings, we were exhausted. We were assigned bunks alphabetically. Our neatly-folded bunks were inspected by our Sergeant and Lieutenant every morning at six.

I recall being on garbage detail one morning when the temperature was minus 52 degrees Fahrenheit. The food in the mess hall was atrocious. In fact, it was so bad I had to go the Salvation Army after supper for a couple of hotdogs.

In addition to aligning and shooting our .303 rifles on the firing range, we learned how to use a variety of machine guns, mortars and hand grenades. We learned map reading and hand-to-hand combat. Above all, we learned to accept orders without question.

The Army changed my outlook on life and I credit it for many of the opportunities that followed. It taught me discipline. I learned to respect the decisions of others and to have confidence in my own decisions as well. It may have instilled a stubborn streak in my character but, in any event, it certainly turned my life around.

February 11, 2010

The Army – Part Two

In part one, I told of my training in the infantry in Winnipeg and Shilo, but stopped short of relating what happened a few days before Japan conceded and the war in the Pacific came to an end.

Our platoon was taken into Brandon to lead a parade and 'show the colors'. As we were heading back to the base, the officer in charge led us to a creek that was hidden from the highway and told us we could have a swim before lunch. The guys started diving in and it was obvious the water was about four feet deep.

Having no concern about the depth, I took a running dive into the water. I hadn't noticed the slight bend in the creek and ended up going head first into a sand bar. I remained conscious but had to be helped out of the water and placed in a jeep to cross the prairie to Shilo. I was dropped off at the Medical Office. There was no one on duty that could help me and I was told to walk to the hospital, half a mile away.

When I arrived, I was told to sit in the lobby. I must have passed out, as the next thing I knew I was in an operating room. A doctor started to put me in a cast and I fainted again. He explained that if I could be suspended from the ceiling he could do a better job than if I were sitting. I asked him to give me a chair so I had something to hold onto. He then tilted my head back and wrapped me in plaster that covered me from my head to the top of my legs. Holes for my eyes, ears and mouth were cut at some point. I was told that the doctor had just recently returned from Europe.

My parents must have been notified because they, and my oldest sister, arrived at the hospital the next day. I wasn't told why they came so soon, but I later wondered if my condition had been considered critical. I didn't make the connection until much later, but when I was in bed in Shilo I experienced what may have been a near death dream. I clearly saw, and can still remember floating down what looked like a large and long pipe. In the distance I could see miles of grass and multi-coloured flowers. I didn't see any people. I didn't tell anyone of the experience at the time and still don't talk about it.

Nurses wheeled me to the front of the hospital to watch the action after the end of the war with Japan was announced. Although I couldn't see too well, soldiers were firing their rifles at the water towers to watch water spewing from the holes.

After I learned how to roll out of bed on my own, I was transferred to Deer Lodge Veterans Hospital in Winnipeg. I must have been sedated as I don't remember the trip. After three months, the first cast was removed, my head was lowered to a normal position, and I was wrapped in another cast. It was finally removed, and I was released from hospital, after another three months.

Maple Leaf Estates – 2010

This year, apart from Hurricane Charley of August 13, 2004, is the strangest in living memory.

It has been freezing since we arrived from the usually frigid north in early January, where the prairies are balmy by comparison. Our usually flowering palm trees in Florida are either dead or hanging on for dear life.

The ponds on the golf course are overflowing and new rivulets have developed to challenge the accuracy of the brave souls who overdress to attack the game.

While Maple Leafers have escaped the unyielding snow storms and devastation of the northern States, one has to wonder what is going on with the weather. To add to stateside problems, the devastating eruptions in Haiti and Chile have shaken the globe from its foundation.

Should we be concerned about the mysterious writings of Nostradamus whose prognostications, it is said, indicate that the world will end in 2012? Is it mere coincidence as well, that the ancient Mayan calendar ends in that year as well?

As we wait with bated breath, let us hope for warmth and sunshine for the rest of this year and the next.

The Ides of March

My Favourite Place

I am glad that Lorna, in this writing exercise, selected our home on the Assiniboine River as her favourite place. That will be my strongest piece of ammunition if, at any time in the future, she, or any of our four kids, suggest we live closer to them.

While she mentions the view and coziness of our veranda, I content myself with starting the day first, making my own breakfast of cereal, coffee and maple syrup waffles. If I'm feeling fit, I'll bring in the Free Press and check the crossword. I sit next to the window to see if there are any deer tracks in the snow or where the returning geese are raising their yearly brood.

Another benefit of the house is my private office in the basement, filled with detailed records of every case I sat on, my written rulings in civil cases and my charges to every jury I had. The walls are covered with Aboriginal art and memorabilia.

In another basement room we have a four and a half by nine billiard table we bought from a rural barber and dismantled and moved to the six houses we have lived in since. Its present resting place was built so a player's cue never hits or is bothered by a wall. The major benefit is that our growing number of grandchildren all learned the game with their parents, making our home a favourite meeting place.

Looking ahead, one possibility is to install a riding escalator, to make my descent to the lower level, and return to the main floor, safer. I have even suggested a live-in maid, but to say the least, the strength of Lorna's response leaves me in no doubt of her position on that subject.

As long as neither of us waivers, our present residence will remain our favourite place and domicile of choice.

March 25, 2010

LORNA HAMILTON

Lorna (nee Hasselfield) was born in Deloraine, Manitoba, the second child of Charles and Irene Hasselfield. Her father owned the drugstore and was the only optometrist in the south-west area of the province.

She graduated with a Bachelor of Arts degree from United College, now the University of Winnipeg, and a Diploma of Education degree from the University of Manitoba.

She's married to the Honourable A.C. Hamilton. Together they have four children, one daughter and three sons, and five grandchildren.

Graduating with a double major in English and Mathematics, Lorna taught in schools throughout the province, latterly in Winnipeg where they now live. An abiding interest was in building houses. She designed and supervised the construction of three homes and is always interested in interior decorating.

When she and her husband winter in Florida, they attend the Maple Leaf Creative Writing class and she decided to try to write a novel, a work in progress over three years, titled The Book of James. *Lorna is a valued participant in our writing group at Maple Leaf since approximately 1991.*

January 20, 2009

It wasn't that he was a black man speaking.
It wasn't that his ancestors were slaves.
It wasn't that he promised he could save us.
It was because he saw a greater day.

The throngs that gathered screamed their approbation.
The elite smiled as they are wont to do.
He dreamed a dream, envisioned greater purpose
And pledged that law was not just for the few.

He said that all our efforts were not wasted.
He saw worlds in a newer, shining light.

He made us all believe that love could triumph.
God give us grace and pray he may be right,
With 'Yes we can' a slogan for all peoples.
God help him to erase this nation's blight.

January 20, 2009

Night Song

Singing softly, softly sighing,
Softly, softly, through the night,
Myriads of stars are shining:
      Blue light.

Singing gently, gently sighing,
Gently, gently, through the night,
Fog is swirling, foaming, twirling:
      Dew light.

Moaning, keening, softly crying,
Moaning, keening, through the night,
Shattered souls with fingers clinging:
      Grey light.

No more sighing, no more moaning,
Softly singing through the night,
Color melding, streaking, fusing:
      Day light.

Blindness

Tell me of the sunset, of the colours and the glowing.
Paint your words with sulphurous hues and get me back to
    knowing
Reds, redeemed with warmth and heat, yellow bands and green.
Mention all the harmonies to make me see God's scene.

Close my eyes to blackness, let my mind create the sight;
See again the glory of a sunset drenched with light.
Paint your words with tints of heaven, show me with pure tones
All the colours that the rainbow owns.

Paint your words with all the hues of heaven when it's blest.
Tell me! Tell me once again and I can dream the rest.

March 2004

Armageddon

Sapphire blue as Heaven's Gate
Jesus waiting there:
Waiting, watching through the night.
Satan gets his share.

Heaven's colours: ruby red,
Yellow, blues and green.
Misty is the dawn's pure light.
Grass with purple sheen.

Solemn dancers jump and writhe.
Hated buglers play.
Trumpets blare in silver tones.
Death in shades of grey.

Multitudes with wreaths of gold.
Virgins pale, deprived.
Noises, clamours, loud and black.
Religions now have died!

Heaven's Gate is closing soon.
Dark blue darkness gleams.
Stars and comets misty now.
Nothing as it seems.
Nothing as it seems.

February 2004

Charley

August 13, 2004. A fateful day! We watched the T.V. from
Winnipeg, in horror, as we realized our homes were disintegrating
and we knew we could do nothing about it. This was not supposed
to happen. Port Charlotte was always secure. Nothing could touch
us. We were inland, away from the coast. The storm was to go
north. Our little enclave was protected from wind by the islands
on the bay. The storms blew down Alligator Alley or up the east
coast; never near us. We had been betrayed!

'Charley is my darling, the only one for me'
The song doesn't apply. No 'darling Charley' here, my friends.
No 'darling Charley' here!
He blew a real mean tune.

'Blow Ye Winds Hi Ho'
Oh, oh! Not a gentle breeze.

'Gentle on my mind'
A blue note! So sad! So blue!

'Blue skies smiling at me. Nothin' but blue skies do I see!'
It gets better and better! Lots of new skies now I see! A new note!

'Home on the Range' and the lot looks as if the buffalo roam, but

'The Green, Green Grass of Home'
Is green in Florida and,

'Everything is coming up roses, just you wait and see!'

February 3, 2005

Metaphors

A metaphor, a word, can be totally absurd,
Be explicit, can be pretty, or be shady.
It never sees the 'like,' 'as to,' 'compare'—oh good night,
This little rhyme is driving me quite crazy.

The dragon lady's icy, most cold-hearted and not nicey,
And her husband is a slimey, little snakey.
Their kids are more moronic than a stone, that's quite Teutonic,
And the family friends are all a little crazy.

Grandmama is just a pet and you certainly can bet
That the scene becomes a zoo. So it's quite funny
When the son-in-law is near, he's a pussy-cat it's clear
And the daughter is a perfect little lady.

I could really carry on and describe the tribe ere long,
But I know that I would bore you all quite silly.
And so I'll close and say that I hope I made your day
If I did, then my 'Metaphor's' a dilly.

The End of the Affair

Winter whispers with its silvery breath
And tells a haunting tale of snowy dreams,
With feathery, filtering shapes and shadowy schemes,
And soft-gleaned whiteness of a silent death.

The snow falls lightly on the travelled paths
And covers up the footsteps made in haste,
To give a grace to walkways strewn with stones,
And soften all the harshness of the past.

The trees take on new life outlined in frost;
And all the myriad branches are defined
With gossamer and lacy breath entwined.
And summer's passion seems a gentler loss.

February 28, 2003

Unto Death

Hold my hand as I go into that dark night alone.
I know that I must go and you can't follow me.
I loathe the darkness and I fear the cold.
Too late to now confess the bitterness I can't condone.

Look into my eyes 'til they no longer see
And know the sightlessness will not decrease.
We loved each other lately, but such pain was there
It blighted much we had together and it shattered peace.

The dark is now descending and the dawn's not near.
I fear all spectres of a sinful past.
I do not plead for passion for passion now is past for me.
Just hold me in your arms 'til the dark glows.

March 2005

JOANNE ALEXANDER

Joanne started life in Toronto Canada. She wanted, at various times, to be a famous skater, a famous actress, well, just a famous something!

Today she is a full time caregiver for her 88-year-old husband. She enjoys writing, painting, and swimming. She still dreams of fame.

C*O*N*T*R*O*L
1/3/9

You may remember that shortly after Hurricane Katrina, we rescued a Belgian Malinois from New Orleans. The breed is often used for police work and is strong, fast and intelligent. We are in our declining years and police work is out of the question as *we* are no longer strong, fast or smart.

Why else would we have given houseroom to Sun-the-Bum?

Complaints have been lodged against us here in the Park. Our neighbors and friends seldom venture into our territory and Greta, our Great Pyr is ashamed to call him brother. For all that, he is still a love. His enthusiasm is boundless, his loyalty unquestionable and to watch him run free in the northern woods is an affirmation of nature's grace and beauty.

Nevertheless, we winter here – in a gated community full of fearful, fragile seniors and S-t-B does *not* fit in well. After his latest escape where he joyously reached supersonic speeds on Selkirk, we were at our wits' end.

I am daily expecting a summons from the Disciplinary Committee. Might we have to put him down? It seems all too likely.

We had paid an enormous sum to have him trained right after we got him but our inconsistency ensured failure. We had tried seven different training collars and restraints to no avail. We had installed chain locks on the doors after he learned how to work the handles. It was *HELL.*

The other night we watched *The Dog Whisperer* on TV. Cesar Millan is like a *magician* and despite the warning not to try his techniques without a trainer, we went ahead and did what he did. The next time S-t-B started barking we made him sit, forced him to lie down, put him on his back, applied pressure to points in his neck and held him there 'till he was quiet. It was amazing and worked immediately. Next we found the spot on his side where a pack leader would nudge him and that worked too. We've only been at this for two days but there has been great improvement.

I will be sixty this year and hope to celebrate my birthday as an *Alpha Dog-Pack-Leader*. It ought to be easy. I've always been a bitch.

Six Degrees of Separation

April 01, 2010

In the beginning there was the Word and the Word
was God and He created the heavens and the earth.

The Holy Bible: Genesis

An absolute; an immutable truth – or is it? Not all agree. There is Islam and the mighty Geechi-Manitou and Shiva and the Pantheon of the Greek and Roman gods and Buddah and governments and tyrants and principalities and powers. Are they all somehow related through *the absolute* of perfect creation or did chance make them all so different and yet so united in their focused determination to seize absolute power?

It is power and control that unites the human spirit. It is the quest of mastery that hones man's accomplishments. History makes it clear. All animals band together. There is always an alpha, a dominant leader. They always mate and fight and love and hate and live and die and shun those unlike themselves. The greatest insult is comparison to that which is most despised.

All animals are self-centered. The virtues must be taught. The vices come naturally. The greater the intelligence, the less need there is for the companionship of others. The greater the intelligence, the greater thirst for understanding.

Above all else we prize the ultimate cachet of exclusivity – the desire to have something that is denied the common herd. We create rules and customs and codes of dress and behavior that identify our place.

The degree of separation is not what is important, but it is a charming distraction and keeps us from dwelling overmuch on the inescapable, fearful absolutes.

Alpha or Omega

Life or Death

Uncertainty

Oblivion

Heaven

Hell

G O D

Sudie's Story

After I'd been working at the Anderson mill for about ten years, a new man came to work on the machines. His name was Arthur Alexander and he was a smart one and a handsome one. All us girls would stand up a little straighter when he'd walk by.

Now, I never thought he'd take a shine to me, but that very first Sunday he came up to me after church and asked, could he walk me home.

I smiled as big and happy as I could and said, "Yes, sir!" and he took my arm. I knowed that very day that he'd be my man for life.

He come up on the porch and set and talked to Mamma an' Daddy like he'd knowed them for all of his life an' he asked Daddy's opinion on some things at the mill – people he should meet an' so forth – so that pleased Daddy fine.

Mama said she'd made chicken an' cornbread and greens and macaroni pie for dinner an' invited him to set down with us. Well he did and he praised her cookin' most highly. Mama took that real kindly an' asked would he come an' eat again next week. She tol' him she'd be makin' ham biscuits, if that took his fancy, and we'd have real sorghum syrup from the home place up to Sunshine.

Well, he just lit up an' said, with that purty white smile of his, "Thank you kindly, ma'am. I'd like that fine."

Not a bit of hem-in an' haw-in 'bout that man! No sir.

An' then Mama she said what a pleasure it was havin' new folks like him in town.

Well… when I went to the mill that night for my shift, it was all over that I had me a beau and it jes' tickled me! I kep' smilin' and smilin' all the time I wuz workin'. Them girls asked me over an' over how *did* I catch him and I jes' smiled slow like an' let on I had some purty cute plans for man-catching. 'Corse, it wasn' nuthin' like that. It was jes' fate. He liked my looks an' I surely did like his!

We'd go for walks some nights along the path by the li'l ol' crick that flowed into the mill pond an' we'd watch the lights of the trains as they went on by the mill and' we'd think out loud what it'd be like to ride on one of them trains, headin' out to someplace new.

But I tol' Arthur I was satisfied with where I wuz, an' I still am. Arthur had influence an' he had it fixed so's we had our own house. We went there straight after church the day we wuz wed. Mama n' Daddy's house wuz one of the furtherest from the mill an' one o' the biggest, but Arthur, he got us a right nice little one just one street up from the mill store an' the barber shop was right on the corner. I wuz so proud of that house! I made the nicest curtains an' I had me my own pots an' a lovely big fry pan – the same one as is out there on my range right now. Arthur had got us a suite of bedroom furniture from a big store right there on Anderson Main Street an' had it delivered. It was somethin' fine I can tell you! First thing I ever made fancy was a crocheted mat for the chiffoneer. They's some flaws in it for I warn't as smart with a hook as I am today, but I've got it yet and you have to look close to see where I lost track of myself.

They talk about sex today like it wuz somthin' they done invented like the moon shots, but I am here to tell you we had lusty love back in them days too. When we got to our house, Arthur he jes' slammed that door shet behint us an' grabbed holt of me like I wuz gonna run away. He had him a jug of moonshine an' he took a big swig of it an' wanted *me* to hev some too but I turned that down FLAT! Gaines an' me had done tried some of Daddy's white lightnin' years afore an' it was NASTY! I didn't tell Arthur that but I tol' him I had brung some of Mama's an' my own home growed Muscadine wine from the grapes in our own back yard. So… then we toasted our health in jelly glasses in our own front room. We wuz that proud!

The wine relaxed me some an' so I was ready for love makin' when Arthur led me to the bed. I knew what to expect o' course, I sorta' think that Arthur tried real hard to make it nice for me. I wuz surprised about a few things… fer intstance, I had a hard job not to laugh as he stood there whilst we were getting naked. He had took off his shirt an' shoes and trousers an' there he stood with one toe stickin' out of his sock an' his big ol' thing stickin' out of his drawers. I turned my back! I didn' want him to see I was jes' a grinnin' at him. It might of made him feel bad. Finally we both got off all of our clos' and we stood there lookin'. It wuz about one o'clock in the afternoon an' HOT. I had pulled down the green shades an' the room wuz' all shady like.

It wuz' obvious what we wuz supposed to do an' *wanted* to do, yet there stood Arthur – looking! It made me MAD. For all he wuz' so smart I wuz' goin' to have to take holt an' begin or we'd never do nuthin! There's books now, so I'm tol' on yer tech-nique! I don' know if what I did was proper or not but I jes went over to him an' put my arms arount him an' stroked his neck an' his lovely curly hair an' then he did the same to me an' finally, by'n'by we laid down on the bed. It was a relief to me I can tell you!

In later years, when he wuz drunk an' mean an' would take me like I wuz some kinda' hoor, I'd try to stay quiet an' I'd look up at the ceiling an' remember how it wuz that very first time, when we wuz both young an' a little bit scairt of lovin'.

Sudie's Story – Ch. 4

1/22/09

The Back Parlor at Number 22 West End Avenue

Sudie cleared her throat and asked, "How many rooms you an' Kenny have to yo'r big ol' house on the hill up there in the North?"

She sat in her brown leatherette recliner rocker in the comfortable back parlor. No one ever used the front parlor except to walk through it on the way back here. The house was welcoming and it was Sudie's pride and joy. There are only five rooms inside but the big, wide front porch, partially screened by vines and furnished with cane back rockers is really another room. So is the area off the kitchen where the family gathers for outdoor meals under the shade of a huge pecan tree.

No one but Sudie ever sat in the brown chair. It was her special corner and she had all her things 'ranged round it, just so. If the pole lamp with the green shade was one inch out of place it had to be put right- and right away! On the wall opposite the chair was a great, big, sepia-colored portrait of FDR, elaborately framed and hung from the picture rail by a gilt swag. It was clearly the most important element in the room. No matter where you sat, Mr. Roosevelt beamed down on you. Beside it and slightly to the right was a framed, faded poster that said, "NRA member" and showed a blue eagle and "US" and underneath, "We do our part."

Sudie wasn't a gun-toting member of the NRA as we understand it today. This NRA of the poster and the blue eagle symbolized

FDR's *National Recovery Administration.* When FDR was elected in 1933 this country was deep in the depths of the depression. Arthur had a job but with five small children he would often take Ken or Linnaeus with him down to the place where they handed out free sacks of flour and pails of lard. Sometimes you could get bread. They had a cow and a flock of chickens in the back yard and grew vegetables. Every year they got a pig and fattened him up for slaughter, then cut him up and salted him down in a big wooden box. That was food for the year. They were the lucky ones. Many people with less luck or gumption were starving on the streets. Kinfolk went to work in the CCC – *The Civilian Conservation Corps* – part of the **New Deal.** It helped to combat unemployment and operated in every US state and several territories. The separate Indian Division was a major relief force for Native American reservations. To Sudie and all poor Americans FDR was a savior who managed to keep the country from utter ruin.

"Well?" she asked again.

"Uh – ten," I said, "and of course, the basement."

She shook her head in disapproval. "Ten rooms an' only one child. Me an' Arthur raised five children in four rooms." I kept my mouth shut. Ken had told me all about those rooms, about going barefoot, about wiring the house for electricity; I'd heard about the out-house and breaking the ice in a water bowl to wash his face in the morning. I stared fixedly at FDR. "Don't you go and spoil that child," she said. "You teach her to do things, chores an' hand work so if ever things go bad again, she'll be able to do for herself. In hard times, no matter what the gov'ment does, it's up to every person to try his best. You understand what I'm sayin'?" I nodded. "Doin' keeps a body from despair. Remember that." I nodded again.

The Fixer

1/17/7

Although it is not commonly known, there are powers that be, who, from time to time, meddle in the affairs of those on Earth. These forces have been variously called the gods, alien invaders and 'other things'. For the purposes of this story, it is necessary only that we understand that they have servants among us, who look and act like humans, but in reality, possess *super powers*. You have no doubt heard of Superman. The force we are discussing today goes by the common, humble name of: ***The fixer***.

On January 12, 2008 at precisely 5:14 pm, a message was sent to ***The Fixer***. Her services were required. ***The fixer*** had not been needed for a very long time, but, as usual, when the call was made, she sprang into action. The master spoke to her, thusly, "A cry has been heard from the great unwashed to the grand pantheon requesting clarification of this question: "WHAT is wrong with today's society???" ***The fixer***, long used to the vagaries of HE who must be obeyed, sought elucidation. "Oh great master," she murmured, for of course, **fixers** do not shout, "What wouldst thou have me do?" HWMBO replied, "Go thou into the depths of the Internet and solicit answers from the multitudes who search thereon. Find from them the heights their souls do reach and yearn for; discover their hopes and dreams, their goals and aspirations. Secure with this knowledge, thou needs must wave *thy magic wand* and **fix** the Earth, for it is plain to me *and* thee that it is in direst need of fixing!"

The fixer sighed, for she had been about to give herself a pedicure, *but,* noble being that she was, she went forthwith to the keyboard of her computer and thereon entered data. Despite the swiftness of her nimble brain and fingers, she was shocked at the *long* hours of boring labor that the task required. At length she had it figured out and sent a voice-mail to the Master saying, "Dear Master; as per your instructions I have made enquiries and, sad to say, the solution is beyond my humble powers. It is all **thy** fault. Thou hast given to the unwashed multitudes the gift of free will, without endowing them with wisdom. For each who howled unto the Internet seeking succor and revenge, there were three more who howled with opposite determination. But, Master, do not despair. I am **the fixer** and thou hast placed thy trust in me. I have studied long and hard and this is what Thee must do to fix the problem."

She waited only nano-seconds before the Master appeared before her. "MUST???" growled the Master. "Yea, verily!" replied *the forceful fixer.* "Thee MUST segregate the planet into cages strong and into each one place those of a group determined. Divide thee those whose vision seeks strong rule from those who would be free. Divide those who hate from those who love and those who meddle from those who do their thing. Separate the rich ones from the poor and the educated from those who cannot learn. Kill all the rest and let the waters of the mighty oceans hide their defects large from view."

"NO!!" roared the Master. "These are all our much loved creatures. We have made them good and bad, strong and weak, beautiful and ugly, smart and dumb. Why dost thou think they cannot live in harmony all together?"

The fixer laughed. "Oh great Master," gasped *the Fixer,* tears of mirth and sorrow commingling on her cheeks, "Who dost thou think thou art? John Lennon???"

VIC MIZZI

Vic was born in 1930 in Sault Ste Marie, Ontario to Italian immigrants. He grew up speaking fluent Italian, part of a family of three boys and three girls. He graduated from the University of Toronto with a DDS and practiced dentistry for 43 years, prior to retiring. Vic has one son, Mark, aged 52, plus one brother and two sisters still living. He has been married to Linda for 25 years.

His hobbies are flying floatplanes, soaring (he has an instructor's license and taught soaring in the Sault for many years), fishing, golfing, playing in a band, traveling, reading, writing, studying languages (Spanish, French, German) and traveling abroad once per year.

He and Linda enjoy six months each year in Maple Leaf.

The Last Violin

His name is Cliff Gutcher. He is an old, retired friend in the last stages of terminal cancer. He is making for me his last violin. The workshop, where he crafts his beautiful instruments is behind his old, clapboard house in an old section of town.

To reach the shop I pass through a "manicured" garden of vegetables laid out with strings, in precise rows. A short, narrow walkway of tiles, bordered in flowers, leads me to the door of a small, red-painted building.

Stepping inside, my nose is assailed by the acrid smell of exotic lacquers mixed with the aroma of rare wood chips as my eyes are immediately drawn to a line of gleaming violins hanging from the ceiling of the ten by twelve room. Behind those instruments I see another row of hooks holding bows, newly strung with horsehair, waiting to be drawn across G D A and E strings.

Between a band saw and sander, a cabinet with open shelves holds neatly stacked blocks of maple, pine and ash, – all dated, aging and awaiting their time to be made into works of art. Cliff tells me that it requires seven years of aging before the wood can produce the quality of sound for which he strives. Hanging on more hooks along the wall to the left are two newly constructed, still starkly pale violins awaiting the many coats of stain and burnishes before hand-carved 'scrolls', tuning pegs and lacy 'bridges' can be attached.

On the last wall, under the only window in the shop I see a workbench, ample in size, but diminished in usable work area by a clutter of the tools of his trade. Sharp wood-chisels of every shape and size imaginable vie for space with rows of screwdrivers, needle-nosed pliers, clamps, brushes and countless bottles of stains and paint

A jig, the exact size and shape of the "Antonio Stradivarius" violin he is building for me holds the 'belly' or top half of the instrument which he has been chiseling out by hand, painstakingly measuring in micrometers it's thickness as he works, with the calipers from his apron pocket.

Approaching the exit, I can't help smiling at the yellowed old poster tacked to the door-a man with a clipped moustache – a young Cliff, reading: "Orvano – master hypnotist and magician now appearing" There are other old photos of him with his banjo and glitzy celebrities of years gone by, all with flowery autographs tendering 'best wishes to Cliff, fellow musician, magician and friend'.

As I step out of the workshop, I shake my head in wonder. What a monument to his memory this man has created! Long after most of us have departed this earth, somewhere, sometime, someone will pick up my violin and peer into the "S" hole to read, just as Antonio did five hundred years ago: FACIEBAT ANNO DOMINI MM111 DE CLIFF GUTCHER PER

Erewhon

Last night I dreamed of Erewhon
A world where all are free
To find their God and talk to Him
'Bout hate and bigotry
There were no priests in Erewhon
No Imams or rabbis there
The people had a private way
With God their thoughts to share
No terrorists lurked in Erewhon
To kill for weird beliefs
And massacre the innocents
Their way to air their griefs
There's but one church in Erewhon
Salvation is it's goal
Devoid of pomp and splendor –
The cathedral of one's Soul
Where is this place called "Erewhon?"
I woke and just laid there
In Butler's book I found it
He said it was — Nowhere

Max – Clone #3

My name is Max and I'm a clone. Actually my full name is Maxfli and I was cloned in this huge factory in the US of A.

My earliest recollection is sitting in a neat box with eleven of my siblings in a shop at a place called 'Maple Leaf Estates'. It was very pleasant there, surrounded by shiny implements and colorful shirts, cosily ensconced with my mates, admiring each other's shiny white skin and dimples without a care in the world! But, alas! Nothing lasts forever.

One day an unshaven lout dressed in garish clothing and a ridiculous tam clomped in wearing evil looking shoes with nails protruding from the soles! After handing the clerk some dirty green paper he stuffed our clean box into a dirty leather bag filled with instruments of torture and filthy towels. Well! That was bad enough, but it got worse – much worse!

A few minutes later, after a long negotiation about something called 'strokes', I was wrenched out of my comfortable bed and placed upon a wooden peg, naked for the entire world to see.

"Wham!" A huge metal club propelled me into the sky, where I could see birds, tops of trees, ponds and a large green area where I bounced down amid shouts of 'good shot man!' from the other ruffians. Another blow launched me skyward again – this time accompanied by foul cursing and insults about my character as I splashed deep into a pleasant cool pond where curious fish welcomed me with kisses on my dimples.

Just as I was beginning to enjoy my new home, an ugly contraption yanked me out and soon I was back on the wooden peg and blasted once more into the blue and on coming down, found myself buried in a sand grave! Was this to be my final resting place, never to see my siblings or even my amorous fish again?

But just when all hope was gone, after a barrage of assaults from a tool I heard called a @#$%*&! sand wedge! I emerged, battered and scarred only to be tossed contemptuously back into a pocket of low class homeless balls marked 'for practice only'.

Once more my future looked bleak until my owner decided to use me on a dangerous par three. Again I was set on the peg and another curse, muttering "don't care if I lose this stupid ball, so here goes." And with that last insult I was blasted into eternal fame! Somehow, after bouncing off a tree and skipping across a pond I found myself rattling in the cup – a hole in one!!!

As I sit on this velvet cushion in the trophy case of a hacker named Mizzi, enduring his bragging and raising of glasses, I revel in the knowledge that long after he and his ilk have departed this world, I will still be here – never again to be battered and cursed upon because of lack of talent. On the contrary, I, Maxfli, will always be spoken of by him and his heirs as 'the finest, truest-flying golf ball ever made'!

I Max, Clone #3, will live forever.

GUY CROMBIE

Guy has been in MLE since 2002. Born in Toronto in 1923, he lived his early life in Northern Ontario at Iroquois Falls and Kapuskasing. At age 10, he moved to Toronto where he has been a resident for most of his life.

He attended Oriole Park School and Forest Hill Collegiate. In 1942 he joined the Army and spent a year with the No. 2 Canadian Army University Course at the University of Toronto training to be a technical officer with the 6th Canadian Army Division. When the 6th Division was cancelled, he re-mustered into the artillery and served in England and Europe with the 4th Canadian Army Armoured Division.

After the war he spent a term at Khaki University near London and returned to Canada to graduate in Civil Engineering from University of Toronto. Guy joined Ontario Hydro where he was involved in the design and construction of hydro, coal fired and nuclear power plants and was the manager of engineering for several large electric power plants.

He is married to Mary Jane and they have four children and seven grandchildren. They divide their year between their cottage on Six Mile Lake, their condo in Toronto, and MLE.

After retirement Guy served as an elected District and Area Councillor for the District of Muskoka and Township of Georgian Bay for 9 years. He is still active on several committees relating to lakefront cottages.

Artist David Milne

A group of seven contempory who lived year round in a small cabin on Six Mile Lake in Muskoka from 1933 to 1939

This celebrated artist, whose works are in the National Gallery in Ottawa, the McMichael Collection, the David Thompson Collection, and Art Galleries across Canada, built a 12 by 16 foot cabin on the south-east shore of Six Mile Lake in 1933. He spent the summers and winters for the next six years in relative isolation, pursuing his goals as a painter. Images of landscape and still life dominate this period. Previously Milne painted in the USA, Canada and was a Canadian Army artist in Europe. Born in 1882 on a farm in Ontario, he became a significant figure in Canadian Art History by the time of his death in 1953, although he seldom made enough money to pay income tax. One his paintings sold for $1,437,500 in 2008.

Like many other Canadians during the great depression, financial and personal difficulties forced him to leave his comfortable life as an artist in Palgrave Ontario for the bush. In April 1933, he and his first wife Patsy had signed a separation agreement. Although Patsy made several visits to Milne's cabin on Six Mile Lake, they never lived together again.

David Milne arrived in Orillia mid May 1933, looking for work at local summer resorts. A week later he found his way to Severn Falls and Big Chute on the Severn River near Six Mile Lake. Partly by design, but mostly by accident, he found the location of his future cabin. He liked the openness and privacy of the lake over the river, it was here that he planned to start his new life and concentrate on his painting.

By mid October 1933 he began to build a small cabin constructed on land rented from the Province of Ontario for five dollars per year. By late December the tar paper shack was ready to move into for the winter. His closest neighbours were two miles away at the Hydro Electric power plant colony at Big Chute. It had a log school for the children at which Milne on occasion taught an art class. The nearest store was at Severn Falls five miles away, where there was a CPR railroad station. In the winter the solitary life suited him just fine and he felt he owned all of Six Mile Lake.

Milne built his cabin on the neck of a small somewhat barren point that had been burnt over many years before. His cabin looked west out over the lake and had small bays to the north and south, and the bush behind him. Milne related that the cabin, made mostly from scrounged materials, cost forty dollars and a lot of misery. The cabin was heated and cooking was done using a stove salvaged from an abandoned hunt camp. For storage, shelves were built across both sides and the end of the cabin. An etching press was located on a work bench in front of the shelves across the end of the cabin. Milne had a cot at the other end together with a small table fashioned from a shipping crate. A hanging lamp gave illumination. Although the water in the pails froze on many a cold night, Milne never found the cabin uncomfortable in either summer or winter.

Although Milne was sophisticated man, the Great Depression forced him to live a hand to mouth existence. He established a small garden that was six foot by ten feet just to the north of his cabin. He grew onions, lettuce, rhubarb, beets, beans, tomatoes and flowers. Although Milne complained about the work to create and maintain his garden such as planting and watering as well a continuing battle against animals who raided his garden, his friends believed he enjoyed gardening, which reminded him of his childhood when he spent time gardening with his mother.

He purchased living supplies from a store in Severn Falls. He usually canoed or skied the several kilometers by way of Big Chute. Larger orders came from Eaton's Department Store. Those items that would freeze were stored in a root cellar dug into the ground that maintained an above freezing environment.

In need of money, he wrote to Vincent Massey and wife Alice in August 1934, to offer them 1000 paintings, which were his life's work, for five dollars each. By 1934 the only works that Milne had sold in Canada were to the National Gallery of Canada and an oil painting to the Masseys of white flowers, perhaps trilliums, placed in a jug in a window sill overlooking the roofs of a small town. Milne needed the $5000 to live and he worried about the safety of his works which were stored in scattered locations including New York, Buffalo, and Big Moose Lake. The remainder were at Weston, Palgrave and his cabin at Six Mile Lake.

Eventually the Massey's bought some 300 paintings at five dollars each, mostly paintings done since his return to Canada. Since it was a fantastic purchase, the Massey's entered into an arrangement with Mellor's Gallery (now Laing Gallery) in Toronto whereby they would offer for sale some of the canvases they had purchased. It was decided that whatever profits were to be made would be shared between Milne and the Massey's, with Massey's share to be turned back into a fund to purchase Canadian Art. This arrangement served the double purpose of securing Milne a fair return on his work, and no less important, brought Milne to the attention of the not very large art collecting public at the time.

This resulted in a steady flow of notes and letters between the Massey's who were now in London and Milne's tiny cabin in the wilderness on Six Mile Lake. Milne described his environment – the tiny cabin's interior, his painting place for the day, the brilliant sunshine on the rocks and the blue waters, or the terror of a winter storm. Some of David's descriptions follow:

- "The first very cold night of the winter, clear, snowy and with a high wind right from the north. Over the windows on this side I have hung two blankets. On the west window I can see the sparkle of frost. As I look steadily at it, I find it hard to believe that I am not looking through it at the sky and the stars. The cabin is banked around with snow, the wind rattles the tar paper on the roof, and inside – this is the miracle – it is warm, light, quiet; the clock ticks, the fire crackles, and the wind makes a whooing sound in the stovepipe. From this one small place in all the wilderness the storm is shut out, here a human being can work, eat and sleep, safe right in the midst of danger." (Milne's letter to Alice Massey December 3, 1935.)

- "Nobody ever made a better Sunday morning than this… The point of rock with pines on it pushing up into the breeze. Blue lake and white pillow clouds. The sweet scent of pine needles distilling in the sun. I paddled over to this island in the morning before the wind got up, brought my lunch – bread and butter, cream cheese, strawberry jam (very nice), a lemon sugar and a cup – I have a wind breaker, the old army coat, and ground sheet to sit on, this pad and pencil to write with, and some sketch paper." (Milne's letter to Alice Massey, July 5, 1935.)

Vincent Massey said: "After reading Milne's letters, as fresh and as tart and vivid as his paintings, you did wish that you could tap for maple sap in Hyde Park or take a canoe ride on the Thames, so descriptive were they of the Canada he loved."

The Massey financial rescue re-established Milne's reputation as a serious artist, and he became better known by the Toronto and Canadian art community.

Milne was educated in Paisley and Walkerton, Ontario and at age 21 went to New York and for the next ten years studied art, worked at art, and met and married his first wife Patsy. He succeeded in having five paintings in the historic Armory Art Show which introduced him to such European painters as Edvard Munch, Henri Matisse and Marcel Duchamp.

After his service in World War I as a Canadian military artist, he and Patsy disappeared in the Adirondacks where he built a house, doing all of the work by himself. However, it was too expensive to hold with the Great Depression on the horizon. He sold it for a small income stream and returned to Canada, living in Palgrave and Ottawa.

At first the Depression did not affect them. Unfortunately the US Bank failure caught up the people who had purchased their house and Milne lost most of his income stream. This ended his marriage and he moved to Six Mile Lake.

Upon completing his cabin, Milne settled into a routine which centered on painting. He would rise at six in the morning and start the stove to prepare breakfast. After breakfast he would haul water from the lake. He would wash the dishes and do any necessary cleaning. Once his chores were complete, he would start to paint until three or four o'clock in the afternoon. Next Milne chopped and split wood, which was his favourite chore, after which he would start to prepare supper. After supper he would pass the time reading and writing or reviewing the day's painting. He always left the dishes until the next morning. Milne usually retired at ten at night. This routine was broken to go for the mail and supplies on Thursday or Friday. He usually canoed or skied the several kilometers to Big Chute. The Angus family was Milne's main social contact. Christmas dinners and overnight stays to see local school plays and recitals were spent in the company of this warm and amusing family.

Visitors to his Six Mile Lake cabin were always an interruption, people from the art world such as Buchanon, Alan Jarvis, Douglas Duncan his art dealer and his wife Patsy, and after 1938 his second wife Wyb. Often the ladies from the Ontario Hydro colony at Big Chute Generating Station hiked to his camp for a picnic. They would do any cleaning or washing of dishes to be done, and Milne would take time to prepare and serve tea to the ladies.

The long cold days of winter and the constant droves of mosquitoes and black flies in the spring caused Milne to work inside, often away from the actual painting material, the landscape. This resulted in spending more time on a painting and he found he could produce larger paintings and night scenes. He often did quick sketches to capture the immediate composition. Colour and lighting effects were recalled when it was time to paint.

Milne travelled more in the late 1930's, visiting his brother Jim in Paisley, the National Gallery in Ottawa, and to Toronto. A meeting with A.Y. Jackson at Mellor's Gallery resulted in a lunch with him, Arthur Lismer and Barker Fairly.

One day in 1937, a young nurse named Kathleen Pavey paddled her canoe by his cabin. They met and became friends. He made frequent trips to visit her at a cottage where she was staying on Tea Lake, which is just above Big Chute. Eventually they fell in love and she became his second wife in 1938, Kathleen was 28 and he was twice her age. With Kathleen in his life, his art began to take on a new turn; it became filled with playfulness and fantasy. Their son was born in 1941 when the artist was 59.

By the spring of 1939 Milne was ready to leave Six Mile Lake, probably influenced by his new wife. In a letter written on August

28, 1938, Milne suggests that he has had enough of the solitary life; "Occasionally the cabin has foiled me and I have felt a strong desire to walk out on it, to leave the clock ticking, the kettle humming on the stove, the pails full of water. The pictures lying in their usual place, everything just as it is, not to close the door, not to look back, or ever think of it again, or remember anything connected to it. Simply go, to make an end, with no feeling except relief, clean free and new, as a snake as it crawls out of its skin."

Milne returned to the cabin for a few weeks in October 1939, to put on a new roof and install new stove pipes. Although he evidently intended to maintain the cabin for a future visit, it was his last visit. In November 1939 he was back in Toronto, living with Kathleen.

The final phase of Milne's painting were landscapes at Baptiste Lake where he built his last cabin in 1948. Suffering from failing health, he had his first stroke in 1952. He died of a second stroke on December 26, 1953.

David Milne Jr. was just 12 when his father died. In addition to his father's art, there was his literary work that had to be referenced to his paintings. In 1996 David Milne Jr. with David Silcox launched a biography, 'Painting Place: The Life and Work of David Milne'. In 1983 David Milne Jr. and his family bought a business, Birchcliff Lodge across the lake from his father's cabin on Baptiste Lake.

BILL O'HARE

Bill was born and brought up in Holyoke, Massachusetts. He is a graduate of the University of Massachusetts in Amherst. He worked in various technical and managerial positions for IBM in California and Massachusetts, retiring in 1993. He then joined a former customer, Commerce Insurance as director of Network Technology and Computer operations, retiring in 2002.

This time retirement stuck. Bill is currently a winter resident of Maple Leaf Estates in Port Charlotte, where he has been active in various athletic, musical and creative activities. In addition, Bill is now president of the Maple Leaf Board of Directors.

Bill has been married to the former Joyce Sefcik for over 47 years. They are the parents of Bill Jr. in Oxford, Mass., Kelly in Germantown, Tenn. and Daniel in Huntington Beach, Cal. They have been blessed with two grandchildren, Jacqueline and Caitrin in Germantown, Tenn.

The War Years

In 1941, there was a popular song titled 'Goodbye Dear I'll Be Back In A year 'Cause I'm In the Army Now'. My father and mother became engaged in 1941. In March he received greetings from the President and was drafted for what was nominally a one-year term. Pearl Harbor and the deteriorating situation in Europe resulted in bi-lateral declarations of war with Japan on December 8, 1941 and Germany on December 11, 1941. My parents had planned to get married in April of 1942 and saw no reason why a triviality such as global warfare should alter these plans. They tied the knot on April 26, 1942.

My father's outfit, the 4th Yankee Division, had been cut up so badly in WWI, that they were held out of North Africa and Italy, and did not see combat until June of 1944 in Normandy. Meanwhile they were dispatched to Myrtle Beach, South Carolina to patrol the beaches looking for submarine based German spies. My father actually found someone wandering the beach, wearing a trench coat and turned him in. Dad wasn't sure what happened to him after that. Considering the trench coat he may have been returned to Hollywood central casting, or charged with committing a felonious cliché.

I'm not sure if there is any truth to the old saying that 'Love Conquers All', but the O'Hare boys waged and won an assault against the obstacles to love. The specific obstacles in early 1942 were the 750 miles between Holyoke and Myrtle Beach. In addition, a no weekend pass policy was in force at the time. The battle plan was simple, effective and almost foolproof. Most weekends my mother and uncle Roy, who bore a strong resemblance to my father, would board a train from Mass. to South Carolina. My father and uncle would exchange clothing in a men's room and mom and dad would take off to a hotel and Roy would impersonate a staff sergeant for the weekend.

This scam worked surprisingly well for several months. Dad's immediate outfit was in on it. Uncle Roy gave a whole new meaning to the term weekend warrior. I believe that the three of them were forty years ahead of their time. They were simply outsourcing a portion of my dad's enlistment, a practice that became widely accepted and admired in corporate America by the early 1980's.

I earlier used the modifier *almost* in describing the perfection of this scheme. Roy actually picked up enough soldiering skills to stay under the radar from Friday through Sunday night. He became a welcome patron of the NCO (Non Commissioned Officers) club. It was there, on a Saturday, that all this came to an abrupt end. He was, as he later recalled, on the receiving end of a crude insult and a physical challenge. One of his father's dictums on how an honorable life was lived rang in his ears.

'... *Don't ever let me hear of you starting a fight.... but by God don't ever let me hear of you walking away from one...* '

In short order the other NCO was being scooped off the floor and taken to the ER. Roy was taken to the brig. The cover-up machinery was quickly mobilized. In less than two hours with the assistance of dad's friends and the cooperation of a sympathetic guard, my dad was in the brig and Roy was at the hotel sleeping it off. My dad was busted from Staff Sgt. to Corporal. After 90 days in the penalty box his rank was restored. Another important side effect of Operation Myrtle Beach was my mother's pregnancy.

I was born on March 25, 1943 shortly before my father shipped out to Europe. The first order of business was a name. Jack assumed I would be named after him, the paternal grandfather. If I've been at all successful in painting a picture of Jack, this is what you should be seeing. A 60 year old man's man. Medium height, broad barrel chested body. A deep voice that rumbled up from somewhere below the diaphragm. A man not to be trifled with by anyone, but particularly by any women in the family. My mother was barely 23 years old at the time. She claimed to be 5' 3" tall, a shameless exaggeration, and I doubt she saw the top side of 110 pounds. When she announced that she was naming her eldest son William, after the father, there were seismic shocks felt through all of Holyoke.

What is difficult to capture about my mother is how fundamentally tough she was. There was a certain look that came into her eyes when angered. It blew away the fiercest scowl ever attempted by a Hollywood tough guy. Clint Eastwood and John Wayne were puny imitations by comparison. The look was backed by a sharp wit, an even sharper tongue and a sense of right and wrong that was unshakeable. The confrontation was loud, verbally brutal and brief. Jack had no idea what he was dealing with. He never had a chance. My mother respected Jack and in her own way she loved him. She was however, appalled by his brand of callous toughness, his insensitivity toward women and the way he raised his boys. She was amazed at how my father emerged from this family atmosphere relatively unscathed. She made it clear that I was going to carry the name of someone she wanted me to emulate and to hell with outmoded traditions. To everyone's credit she made sure that I got to spend as much time with Jack as we both wished until he passed away five years later.

My father's outfit, the 26th Infantry Division, bypassed England entirely and was shipped directly to France. They landed at Cherbourg and Utah Beach on September 7, 1944. Most of what I know about my dad's service record was learned by surreptitious eavesdropping as a young child. Like many returning combat veterans he was reluctant to talk about his war experience with anyone except for a few fellow Yankee Division veterans who had served together in Europe. Once in a great while, three or four of them would gather over a few beers and quietly talk about the war in our living room. This would take place well after my bed time. Sending me to bed didn't mean I fell asleep. It was a low profile way of tuning in adult conversation without my presence inhibiting their discussions.

The stories were low key, told in monotones, punctuated with sporadic laughter. The happiest stories often involved successful foraging expeditions. One of their comrades named Solly accomplished culinary miracles with a few potatoes, an egg, some flour and a GI mess kit. The potato latkes Solly produced appeared to be one of the War's highlights for these guys. I got the impression these types of memories detracted from the ugliness around them and formed a filter that helped soften the memories. Were it not for the late night eavesdropping, I would not know my father received the Bronze Star combat medal. I believe his reticence was based on the fact that he found war ugly with absolutely no redeeming qualities. I also know that he accepted the war as necessary.

He did occasionally critique the portrayal of the war. He considered most war movies to be an almost criminal misrepresentation and technically inaccurate. People didn't die as quietly or cleanly as portrayed by Hollywood. Troops didn't advance in a straight line separated by few feet. That technique would create a field day for automatic weapons fire. The only movie to receive a partial benediction for its accuracy was "Battleground", a portrayal of the Battle of the Bulge focusing on one outfit's experience of Germany's last convulsive gasp that resulted in more casualties on both sides than any other European campaign. The movie is still available on services such as Netflix. The director, William Wellman was a World War I veteran. The screenwriter Robert Pirosh, received an Oscar for best screenplay. Mr. Pirosh was not only a veteran but he had fought in the Battle of the Bulge. The involvement of these two lent an unusual level of veracity and authenticity to the film. During one scene, propaganda leaflets are being rained down on the troops during a snow storm. Some soldiers are seen quietly walking around collecting the leaflets. There is scattered quiet laughter in the theatre. My father later asked if I noticed and understood. I replied '..*yeah I kind of noticed... but, no I didn't understand...*'. My father grinned'...*The laughers were all vets...toilet paper was in short supply... leaflets were an OK substitute...*'

The effect of 199 days of combat on a person is impossible to gauge. Based on observing the war's impact on other vets my father seemed to handle it very well.

It seemed to manifest itself more in his attitudes than his actions. His views on many revered institutions were altered by experience. He viewed the Red Cross, for example, as a glorified dating service for the officer corps. Political institutions were highly suspect. The only time he ever lied to me was his promise, based on my badgering, to teach me to shoot. The best parts of my dad never got touched. He had a faith in God that I envy to this day. He attended Mass virtually every day of his life. In spite of, or maybe because of this, he was one of the earthiest, least judgmental people you could ever meet.

Game Day

". ...It's not a matter of life and death. It's a hell of a lot more important than that!"

Attributed to former Boston College and
Notre Dame coach Frank Leahy.

The atmosphere in the locker room was tense and filled with apprehension. The sound of puking brought on by pre-game jitters had faded. We sat on the hard wooden benches listening to one of Coach Flanagan's legendary pre-game pep talks. He was pacing and whirling in the front of the room like a hyperactive child in the grip of a sugar high; the volume of his voice and emotional content of the speech moving upward in tandem. His voice continued to rise as he accused our opponents of all manner of evil. He implied that the outcome of today's game would affect the rest of our lives. A future filled with honor and public admiration or wallowing in shame and the venomous contempt of the entire town. It was up to us. Coach was into his wind up, red faced, screaming "...I wouldn't let these goddam sons of bitches kick my ass with my own mother sitting up in the stands... watching me get the crap kicked out of me!" The coach, his voice catching in his throat, was so moved by his speech he seemed on the verge of a breakdown.

The team was growling, groaning, and collectively scraping their cleats on the cement floor like a herd of bulls preparing to charge. As usual I felt like the only one in the room unaffected. I bit down hard on the inside of both cheeks. The pain caused my brows to knit and my forehead to wrinkle. I hoped that this would simulate the right level of focus and rage that Flanagan's war homilies were meant to create. I had my own way of getting my juices flowing and my adrenalin into overdrive. The key was the first hit of the day.

We lined up to kick. Four thousand vocal fans screaming in support. Westfield, in red, was the receiving team. We, in purple and white, were kicking. The sun was bright. It was a slightly cool and cloudless October afternoon. The sweet smell of freshly cut grass was mingled with the sharper scent of lime. The whistle blew, the booming sound of foot meeting ball, a jolt of adrenalin and I was off and running. About 20 yards down the field I cut sharply to the left, closing in on the return man as three of my teammates simultaneously hit the ball carrier. At the same time number 53 launched himself at me. Seeing that the tackle had been made I returned the blow with every ounce of strength that I had. That first hit was always magic. Butterflies disappeared. The sound of the crowd faded away. My entire being was now focused on the game.

We rocked back and forth during the first quarter. Westfield took a 6 point lead eight minutes into the first quarter. Early in the second quarter we had the ball on the Westfield 43. Dave Barret, our quarterback, took the snap from center. He faded back to pass. Everyone was covered. The protection began to collapse. Just as he released a desperation heave, he was hit hard by a blitzing linebacker and a defensive end. As tackles go it could be described as mean but clean. Dave's head smashed into the turf. He appeared a bit woozy as he headed back to the huddle. His eyes, slightly unfocused, swept the huddle.

"Anybody watch the Lone Ranger last night." Dave asked.

"Dave, what in the Christ are you talking about?"

Dave looked puzzled. "I just can't remember how it ended".

"Dave, are you OK," asked Don Olds our wide receiver.

"I just need to know how it ended." was Dave's irritated reply.

"Ref... Time out!" I yelled.

The team trainer came out. As Dave continued to ramble on about the Lone Ranger the trainer led Dave off the field and Coach sent out our number two quarterback Ed Kovak. We were all comfortable with Ed. In addition to being our backup QB he was our starting strong safety and a cool customer. He lacked Dave's slingshot arm but was a smart, competent backup who knew how to run an offense.

Ed called a nice mix of plays, mostly runs, and got us down to their 22. Having repeatedly pounded the left side of Westfield's line, Ed showed why we had faith in his play selection. He called for a counter sweep right. Ed took the snap from center and pivoted a half turn to his left. He faked a handoff to the fullback heading off tackle. Westfield, having been repeatedly pummelled on the left, reacted to the fake. Meanwhile, in the graceful but violent choreography of football, three things were happening simultaneously. I took off at a 90 degree angle from my right guard position. Staying low and moving to my right parallel to the line of scrimmage. Ed took another half turn to his left and flipped the ball to Tommy Wrobleski, the left halfback, now barrelling toward the right end. Westfield's defensive end did his job. He ignored all of the activity on our left and kept his position protecting the right outside against our attempted sweep. I could see his eyes narrow as he drifted out and saw Tommy. His discipline was to be rewarded as he turned in to cut off the runner. Suddenly his eyes got big as he saw me appearing out of nowhere. I slammed directly into the middle right side of his body, driving him out of the play. Tommy cut inside and streaked 22 yards to the corner of the end zone for the touchdown. Ed threw a quick out to the tight end for 2 more points and we took an 8 to 6 lead.

After a couple of uneventful possessions the half ended and we returned to the locker room. Flanagan, as usual, was unhappy with our first half performance. He staged an emotional rant that was totally devoid of any useful direction. No word was offered, nor were any questions asked about Barret's condition. It was considered bad form to ask about the injured until the game was over. All we knew was that Dave was not present.

We were the receiving team as the second half began. On the third play of the half Ed got nailed on a quarterback option. He came to the huddle looking OK but a little puzzled. The huddle fell silent as we waited for Ed to call the play. Looking befuddled and even slightly amused he said, "I don't know how to call a play…but I think I can remember how to run them."

All eleven players had the same thought. Ed's bell had been rung, the quaint 60's euphemism for a concussion. There was no realistic substitute for Ed. The pudgy sophomore who was our nominal third string QB was hopeless. A group decision was reached with neither debate nor discussion. Butch Crane, one of our captains, turned to Don Olds the flanker and snapped, "Donny call a play!" Don barked out, "Pro set thirty eight sweep on two." A flicker of relief and recognition passed over Ed's face. "I can run it."

"Then let's go before we get called for delay of game." I said. Ed executed flawlessly. We picked up a solid 4 yards. Our confidence and resolve were reinforced.

In less than 40 seconds, with no real discussion we had reached consensus. A second concussion was not going to stop us. We immediately redistributed responsibilities. No one saw any reason to inform the coaching staff of our decision. For the rest of the afternoon Don called plays and Ed ran them. We even managed another score in the fourth quarter. As subs came into the huddle they were given a cursory explanation and told to keep their mouths shut. They did. Our defence held Westfield to a scant 89 yards and no points in the second half.

Fifty plus years later, other than a handful of players directly involved, no one was aware of what went on that day. We never discussed it with anyone outside that circle. Today I look back with an unresolved combination of pride and horror on what we did that day.

01/26/2012

JIM SHIRLEY

Jim was a long time participant in the Writers Group. He is married to Sally and they have been residents of Maple Leaf for over 12 years. Jim was born in Cochrane, Ontario and spent 35 years of his life in that area. He began his working career in a wholesale grocery business with his father, then bought his father's garage and became a Ford dealer. He left that business to run a timber limit north of Cochrane, and then progressed to life insurance, before enlarging his practice to include general insurance in Barrie, Ontario. Jim retired in 1995 and keeps active in Maple Leaf with woodworking and many other activities.

Near Death Experiences

I have had a couple of times when I consider myself lucky to be still alive. I operated a pulp cutting operation at mile 103 north of Cochrane, Ontario, and while there the last year I bought three sleigh bodies which I used for sleeping quarters. They had been used by Alex Hennessey when he had had the tractor train hauling building supplies for the Mid Canada radar line built by the federal government during the fifties. The units were well insulated and an oil heater would be ample to keep the crews warm in the coldest weather.

I had such a heater in my sleigh body which I used as an office as well as my sleeping quarters. I did not have a proper oil tank, but simply used a forty-five gallon drum of fuel oil elevated on a rack which gravity fed my stove. When the drum was dry, we simply rolled another drum up a pair of two-by-fours and hooked up the feed line to my stove.

One day I had instructed the chore boy to change my oil drum as it was dry, which he did during the day. When I came in that night, I went to light the space heater. As was the custom, I turned the valve to open the fuel line, waited a few seconds, and then threw a burning kleenix into the heat chamber. To my surprise, the resulting explosion blew me straight back against the wall opposite and I sat there dazed for a few minutes. I was very lucky that there was not a greater explosion and a fire ball from the stove. Everything was quiet, I was also very fortunate that I had waited such a short time to light the stove, not allowing more gasoline into the heat chamber. The chore boy apparently had put a drum of gasoline on the rack instead of fuel oil. I was not seriously hurt, just a few bruises where I had hit the wall. I can assure you that I shut off the gasoline line as soon as I was able to be on my feet, and then sopped up the gasoline inside the heater.

The next memorable experience happened not long after. I had placed a few men cutting black spruce for pulpwood about seven miles distance from my main camp, as it was a particularly good stand of timber. I traveled four and one half miles along the right of way of the railway track and then cut back through the bush three miles to the stand. These men lived in bush camps which I had designed and built in sections so that we could take them in on a swamp buggy trailer attached to a Bombardier, and they could sleep in them at night. These cabins were 12 by 16 feet, and would sleep four men. The floor was pre-fabbed in two pieces, the walls in four and the roof in four. When we arrived at the place where they were to be set up, we simply screwed them together.

I had walked up there to scale the wood the men had cut, leaving fairly early in the morning on a bluebird day and walking the trail where we had taken the cabins up with the swamp buggy. I finished my work about two in the afternoon and started back down to the main camp, seven and one half miles away.

Not long after leaving their camp it started to snow, getting heavier as I walked. By the time I reached the railway track the snow was so deep along the trail that I could not walk on it, it was too heavy. It was not terribly cold, about five degrees Fahrenheit. The extra exertion I had to expend on walking in the snow was beginning to tire me, but I had four and one half miles to go. It was dark by this time and the snow just kept on falling.

I walked out to the tracks, hoping I could walk along it, but it too was heavy going. I walked just outside the rails, but there it was too deep. I tried walking inside the track, but with the same result. I tried walking with my feet completely on the rail, but that was too slippery. I could not get any traction and I was afraid of falling and hurting myself on the track, which was very slippery with all the new snow on it. The only way I could make any headway was to place my heel on the rail and my toe in the snow beside it to achieve any thrust in each step, and then I had to take very short steps to keep my balance. Every once in a while, I would come to a patch where the snow looked shallower and I would try walking beside the rails, but this lasted only a few feet and then I had to revert to my heel on the rail again. It was extremely slow going, doing only about a mile every hour and I was tiring quickly as the snow kept growing deeper and deeper. The snow looked so soft and enticing to lie down and rest, but I knew the result of that – you never wake up if you do lie down. I did fall a couple of times, once bruising my knee on the rail but with no serious damage. It was easy to mark my progress because there were mileage signs every mile along the track so I knew where I was at all times. Had it not been for those signs, I may have just given in after a few hours, but they told me I was coming close to my destination. I had nothing to eat or drink, as I thought I would be back at the main camp after a short seven and one half mile walk. The soft snow looked so inviting, but I repeatedly told myself to ignore it and keep on trudging. It was a very dull time, walking, walking, walking but I thought of nothing else but finishing the ordeal. I couldn't allow myself to think of quitting and I was in good shape, having walked many long distances in the previous few years. I was becoming thoroughly exhausted but I told myself I had to keep going.

Finally, I came into sight of the lights of the camp, and I can't tell you how good they looked when I finally arrived, but I couldn't sit down. I had so programmed myself to walk that I just could not stop, pacing around the cookery for forty-five minutes before I could finally sit and eat something.

Celebrities

He was a shy, quiet, pimply-faced lad who had few friends, who could lose some baby fat, and who talked with a slight accent as if from a strange country. He was an excellent violinist who, being pushed by his parents to take up music was very willing to do so. He was a good student, regularly coming near the head of his class with his high marks. His elementary schooling had been at a rural school just outside Cochrane, but when it came time to attend high school, he had to come to town. He was present at very few dances, making me believe that his parents were not concerned about his social life or that he was just anti-social. I believe his parents were very strict, being farmers from eastern Europe who had little education themselves. I am sure they were determined to see that their only son received the best schooling possible.

He was in the class ahead of me, my sister Frances's year, and I think he took a bit of a shine to her. He thus became a friend of mine during the day because he had to go home to the farm after school. I left for boarding school the next year and did not see him for several years.

I was staying at the King Edward Hotel in Toronto with my parents when I saw him running the elevator. He said "Hello, Mr. Shirley" and I recognized his face and said hello to him. We chatted until I departed the elevator, me trying to place his name. I knew he had been a student at Cochrane High but couldn't think of his name.

When I came in that evening, I waited until the elevator he had been running came to the ground floor, took it, and asked the new operator what the previous operator's name was. He said I would have to ask the floor manager that question. After a two dollar bill was put in his hand, he told me, 'Val Lesso'.

The next day I made a point of waiting until he was near the end of his shift, then invited him for a cup of coffee, anxious to find out what he was doing in the big city. We met in the coffee shop and he told me that he was really looking forward to travelling to the Banff School of Fine Arts to study violin that summer. He was disappointed with his musical career up to that point but hoped that this would open some doors for him. He said he was frustrated with his advancement in playing in spite of his continued studying but felt that he still had a career in music.

I next heard of him, not concerning music, but about bank robberies. He called himself Steve Suchan and had teamed up with Lennie Jackson carrying out daring armed heists of banks. He had sold his violin and bought a handgun at a pawn shop. They were not averse to striking a bank employee if they did not do what they wanted, or firing shots over their heads to scare them. The two later joined Alonzo Boyd and Willie Jackson when they escaped from prison in 1951. They would all meet at Steve's house in Cabbagetown to set up their robberies, and to lay low when necessary. The four next pulled off the biggest robbery in Toronto history, splitting up the money. Lennie and Steve went to Montreal while Alonzo and Willie stayed at Steve's parent's home in Toronto. Steve's father told the boys they could stay with them and lay low, that he had an excellent hiding place for the money. The next morning, Steve's father was gone and so was the money. Like father, like son.

In March, 1952, Steve and Lennie were driving in Toronto when they were stopped by the police. They proceeded to shoot at the police car, mortally wounding Detective Tong and seriously injuring Detective Perry. Perry lived but Tong subsequently died, but not before naming Suchan as his killer. The manhunt was far reaching, extending to Montreal where the police knew Suchan had an apartment. They waited for him, and when Suchan returned, they shot him as he reached for his gun. They also moved into Lennie's apartment and captured him after a lengthy shootout. The two survived and were returned to Toronto to stand trial. The other two members of the gang were also finally caught and incarcerated in the Don Jail. The four of them escaped in early September 1952 and holed up in a barn near Yonge and Sheppard. They were captured when reported by suspicious neighbours on September 16, 1952. Suchan and Lennie Jackson were sentenced to death for the murder of Detective Tong. They were hung back to back on December 16, 1952 at the gallows in the Don Jail. Boyd and Willie Jackson were given life sentences and were paroled in 1966.

March 22, 2007

Dan

I had to think about what to write on the subject of illegal activity. I didn't want to incriminate myself, so I picked story in which I couldn't be arrested.

This tale takes place years ago, before I was married. Being a single young buck, leading a carefree life, I was out driving with three of my friends after dark in my convertible with the top down on a beautiful summer evening in Cochrane, Ontario. I don't think any of us were twenty-one, old enough to drink. One of the boys sitting in the back seat was Dan, the son of the local judge. Beside him was the fifth passenger, an open case of twenty-four beer, which we happened to be drinking as we drove south of town. My home town being a small settlement of forty-five hundred souls was the sort of place where you knew everyone. There were very few newcomers to town, most of us had been born and raised in Cochrane and we loved the life.

We were just a few miles down the south highway when a police car drove up beside us and gave the signal to pull over. In those non-violent days, the police car would park in front of you when he stopped you, so you could not step on the gas and leave him in your dust. As the officer parked his cruiser, Dan, being the son of a judge, was quite worried about being stopped with the beer in the car. He hoisted the case of beer at the ditch, trying to cough when it hit the ground. Unfortunately, he missed the case striking the grass by quite a bit, so you could hear the crash of the bottles hitting the gravel, and then Dan gave a very long, loud HUH HUH HUH HUH. The policeman, being alone in his car must have missed the whole action, as he simply walked back to my car, shone the flashlight over the side windows, looked at Dan and said "Nervous tonight, Dan?"

Those were the days before breathalysers, so he could not do any roadside test on us, and with the top down, it was pointless for him to stick his head in the window, which was up anyway. Seeing nothing wrong, he went back to his cruiser.

I will leave it up to you to decide whether you think we left the beer in the ditch or scampered over and retrieved the unbroken bottles.

December 4, 2008

ELIZABETH (BETTY) McKENNELL
May 29, 1929 to November 19, 2011.

Betty McKennell died peacefully at the Tidewell Hospice in Port Charlotte, FL on November 19. She was born in Toronto, Canada on May 29, 1929 to William and Ellen Cook.

After graduating from East York Collegiate, she graduated from the Toronto Teachers College, and began her career as a Primary Specialist, first in Toronto and later in Clarkson. Still later she studied the Montessori System, and was a Montessori teacher in the Twin Cities for nearly 25 years.

She is survived by her husband, Thomas, and her two children, Judith Ellen Speltz and John William, and four grandchildren, Thomas Speltz, and Allison, Alex, and Ashley McKennell.

Betty and Tom lived in the Twin Cities from the summer of 1972 to 1996, when Tom retired from the faculty of the Univ. of MN in early 1996. We rented in ML for 3 months that winter, and then bought our present home on Nanaimo Crescent, and became seasonal residents until the present time.

For Want of a Shoe . . .

While driving along the highways and by-ways of towns and cities I have become increasingly aware of a puzzling sight – 'lost shoes', or more correctly 'a lost shoe'. On the boulevards, in the gutters, or on the side of a country road, one sees any number of these shoes in many sizes, shapes and designs.

A child's baby shoe– perhaps tossed playfully out of the window as the tot became bored with the long drive while strapped in a car seat. One can imagine the hours spent by the mother trying to figure out what happened to that new shoe. One finds many sneakers in various stages of wear that may have fallen out of a backpack or a bicycle basket, but more likely teasingly thrown from a school bus. However, many of these seemingly 'lonely' shoes leave one to speculate on how they came to be where they were, and how the owner is coping with the loss.

An almost new Florsheim oxford was obviously owned by a man of distinction. It is amusing to picture a well-dressed businessman, briefcase in hand, approaching his office minus one shoe. A high-heeled dancing sandal with rhinestone straps no doubt belonged to a ballroom dancer, swathed in chiffon and feathers, now trying to dance on the toes of the foot sans shoe. A sturdy, sensible, teacher's clod-hopper, in brown of course, makes one think of the discipline problems encountered as students focus on the foot wearing only heavy-duty hose. The white leather hospital issue may have been tossed at a patient by an angry Nurse Cratchett. And could that one red shoe have been dropped by Dorothy on her way to Oz? Most puzzling to me was the sight of a biker's big black boot. Somewhere a Hell's Angel is speeding along the highway astride his motorbike with one very cold foot.

As I continued to note these odd shoes I began to conjure up in my mind the possible distressing consequences of all these losses. I was thrilled to observe that a foot-saving solution to the problem may have been developed. A new department has been created. It is the Department of Lonely and Lost Shoes, referred to as D.O.L.L.S. A team of very dedicated individuals is responsible for collecting and displaying the said shoes. They have come up with an interesting and unique plan. As they gather these lonely lefties and righties, they are fastened to a tree in close proximity to the area where they were found in hopes that the owner will retrieve the lost item, and once again walk straight and tall. More and more of these 'shoe trees' are appearing. At this time it is not clear whether this is due to the population increase or some other factor—perhaps growing personal carelessness.

It is most reassuring to know that the government in its omnipotent wisdom has seen fit to initiate this needed service for its cash-strapped citizens. You may expect to receive a phone call or a mailing to solicit your support of D.O.L.L.S. I urge you to earnestly consider your support of this worthy cause.

1/15/2004

Letter-Speak

The other day I received a notice, read it, answered it and then realized that I had responded automatically to what I have come to call letter-speak. The communication to which I refer did not begin with 'Dear Betty' or 'To Betty' or even 'To whom it may concern', but simply FYI ending with the request – return in SSE, ASAP – and I dutifully replied! I began wondering if we have become a people so busy and with so little time that we no longer use our beautiful language when corresponding with others. This became my main thought as I reflected on what had been the first letter-speak – that I could recall.

As a child I remember seeing the letters WPA on many public works and I was never clear on the meaning of the letters. Then along came World War II now known as WWII, and we all spoke of the GI, RCAF, WAC, and soon we knew that they all needed R&R. I'm sure that the father of our country was not referred to as good old GW but we all remember FDR, DDE who headed the ETO, JFK, RFK, MLK, and LBJ.

Of course this letter-speak can be rather confusing and one must take care not to confuse the NAACP with the NCAA or the SPCA, the AARP with AAA or AA. One must also be up on the college abbreviations – IU, OSU, UCLA, USC etc. Anyone who attends meetings is quite aware of the use of letter-speak. Those not in the know are often left out of a conversation. Do you recognize AACP, NEA, NRA – not to be confused with the IRA – or the PTA? And how about the GOP, FDP, BSA or the GSA?

I was deep in thought about this growing tendency as I prepared the re-cycling. The sharp edge of a can slit my finger and even I knew that a trip to the hospital was necessary. As I entered the ER I hoped that a good DR and RN with lots of TLC would assure me that a trip to the OR would not be necessary. While there I made an appointment to see a GYN and I wondered if he would DC my taking HRT?

Returning from the hospital I prepared a BLT to be washed down with a PBR, while listening to a CD, then settled down to watch a DVD. It was pleasant to relax after working 24/7. I suddenly remembered that I had a friend who was arriving that afternoon at the SWF Airport. I quickly jumped into my SUV heading to Terminal A – PDQ. She was on a KLM flight, ETA 5:30 EST. On the way home we picked up some KFC and debated between TCBY or DQ, deciding on both! The evening was spent watching TV – choosing PBS instead of ABC, CBS, NBC, or CNN.

I am now off to BAM to pick up a wonderful book on the joy of writing prose as they did in the olden days!

2/5/04

Yes Madam

Many years ago, or as my children say, in the dark ages, I worked in a large department store on the weekends along with other college students. We considered ourselves lucky to have a little job that gave us spending money and that was also quite enjoyable. Being 'part time employees', we were given the 'gopher' jobs and were shifted to different departments when there was a sale.

One memorable Saturday I arrived and was taken from my usual 'College Togglery' area to the women's blouses. There was a huge sale event and before the store opened we were instructed to unpack all the special purchase blouses and stack them neatly on three very large square counters which were placed in the middle of the area. The bell announced the store opening and we moved to one side as the hordes of wild-eyed women frantically grabbed at our neat tables soon turning them into three mountains of blouses. The supervisor watched to make sure that we were busy and directed me to patrol the dressing rooms, assisting customers if necessary.

The long rows of dressing rooms were all occupied and one could hear the grunts and groans as clothing was removed and the new, usually too small item was struggled into. One woman wiggled a hand out her room asking for help. I slowly entered the little cubicle and beheld a rather intimidating customer who had certainly expected to have the manager take care of her needs, not some brash college student. Standing there in a bra-38 long, atop rolls of avoir de pois, I tried to look only at her rather snapping eyes. Claiming that the blouses were all mis-sized she ordered me to find some just like the 25 she had on the chair and on the floor and make sure that they would fit her. I scooped up the goods and headed back to the melee of customers who were literally plowing through the stacks. Throwing the blouses into the mess I found a friend and rolling my eyes I muttered the situation and together we began to hunt for similar blouses and managed to find a few. I decided to let the woman steam a little and just strolled back to the dressing room area. To my surprise I beheld the customer standing outside her room in all her glory waving her arms. "You took my own good blouse with you!" she snapped

"So sorry madam," I said as I pushed the new blouses at her. "Try these on and I will be right back". My friend saw me hurrying back and I told her what had happened.

"You're doing a good job, girls, keep it up," the manager said as she walked by. We both looked at the piles of blouses most of which were white, as was the lost one. We started looking and then started laughing. This was like looking for a needle in a hay stack. We worked our way through the bargain hunters giggling as we went and began tossing blouses right, left and center trying to find one with a soiled collar and definitely tattle-tale gray. It was becoming a monumental task. My one concern was that another super shopper would scoop up the blouse and head for the dressing rooms. Still trying to contain our laughter the light bulb finally went on and we realized that her blouse would be the only one without a sales tag on it. Keeping an eye on the grabbing hands we went as fast as possible and eureka, there it was in all its icky glory. With my prize held high I made my way back to the room. "Sorry to be so long but the crowds are even larger now. Here is your blouse; may I help you with anything else?" Giving me a withering look, she handed me a blouse that I'm sure would not have covered Twiggy and said that she would be right out. I carefully removed the unwanted ones and headed for the cashier who would ring up the purchases. When lunchtime arrived I regaled my fellow part-timers with the story. I wonder now if the woman could actually wear the blouse tucked in or as an open shirt. No doubt it was returned the next day!

3/4/04

Election

It's over and WE WON! Already forgotten are the meetings, the planning, the phone calls, the endless talking. Now a new era begins, one that our mothers would never have believed would or could happen. A president who has defied tradition, would stand up for the rights of children, extend health care, terminate the never-ending war, and hopefully would lead us into a brighter future.

When the letter from the White House arrived by special mail I was delighted, thinking that it was a standard thank you for the work I had done over the past 26 months. To my utter amazement I was invited to meet with our newly elected President, along with others I am sure, to be thanked and encouraged to continue the good work for the next election.

I arrived in the capital, quite aflutter and hopefully dressed appropriately in a pant suit. I was ushered in, alone, to the Oval Room that really is oval but not nearly as large as it appears on television. The President was seated behind the desk and rose to shake my hand. After the usual pleasantries, the weather, the family, the state, I wondered what was coming next. I soon found out.

I had been invited to consider an appointment to work in the White House. I was completely taken aback. Me, in the White House, daily? Instantly I wondered what that position would be. Perhaps head usher who arranges the daily activities of the first family overseeing their comings and goings. Perchance I could be in charge of the male and the female interns, ensuring that they stick strictly to their jobs and resist the temptation to 'visit' our chief. Of course I might be asked to take guided tours through some of the areas. Oh, the possibilities were endless. This was truly overwhelming.

I suddenly snapped back to reality and realized that the President was speaking about the endless coffee parties, cocktail parties and dinner parties that I had hosted to garner votes, thus displaying my ability to cater and prepare for guests. The President stood, shook my hand saying that it was hoped that I would consider being the sou chef for the family. Oh my, that would be exciting, exacting and exhausting.

I accepted.

I left the President to the task of running the country. I was smiling and feeling giddy as I walked along the fabled halls to the heart of the structure – the kitchen. I was met by the head chef, tall, broad and apparently a lover of his own food. Suddenly he poked my arm then began shaking me! "Stop," I said and tried to move away.

"Wake up, wake up, you are dreaming out loud." It was Tom, I was in bed.

"Please let me go back to sleep," I mumbled, "I was about to have a tour of the kitchen and be told how to prepare chittlins, black eye peas, fried chicken and watermelon!"

Superstitious? Not Me!

I grew up in a loving and caring family. I had a happy and carefree childhood, not realizing that this time was the result of careful attention to many superstitions followed religiously by my mother and relatives. Most of these beliefs were brought over from Ireland years before.

I was invited to a friend's home and was very surprised upon walking into the kitchen, that I did not feel the crunch of salt on the floor. Surely her mother knew that one always threw salt over the left shoulder if some grains were spilled.

My mother was a great entertainer, giving parties and dinner parties. I remember on one occasion a relative dropped in just as we were about to eat. There were twelve sitting at the table. My mother immediately jumped up, giving her seat to my uncle, and then almost danced around serving and rushing back and forth to the kitchen, not joining the circle. I was then requested to have my dessert in the den so that my mother could join her guests and there would only be twelve seated.

To me, normal activities were as follows. When the moon is full, turn over your handbag. On New Year's Eve after welcoming in the year with noise-makers outside, a dark haired man must enter the house first. If giving a hand-bag as a gift one has to put a coin in the pocket. You may put a hat on a chair, on your head or on top of a lamp but never on a bed. When walking on a sidewalk the man is always on the outside. If not the wife is up for sale. An itchy palm means money. An itchy ear, you are being talked about! A horseshoe placed over a doorway must be upside down to keep the good luck from falling out.

I could recite many that to me seemed quite logical but as my circle of friends grew I found that many of our superstitions were theirs also but with opposite meanings.

Thus I have shrugged off the mantle of superstition knowing that my fate is in my hands.

I apologize for being tardy. I left my keys on the counter and had to go back into the house. After counting to 10 and turning around 3 times, I was once again on my way.

JEAN WRIGHT

Jean is the mother of two sons both of whom are in the arts. She has one grand-daughter who at eight years of age is totally bi-lingual in both English and Mandarin. Jean came to Canada in 1952. Her main interests are theatre and gardening.

A Worm's Eye View

Earlier that morning Androgynous had again cautioned me about what was up there. Today however I felt venturesome. I was bound and determined to find out what *up there* was all about. I was tired of being in the dark. I was now two inches long and strong enough to take care of myself. I'd had a good meal of lovely, juicy, bacteria knowing I would need all the energy I could muster to propel myself to up there.

I began my adventure by putting myself in an upright position. Then I started to twirl my body around like a cork screw. I twirled and twirled. The more I twirled, the more momentum I achieved until finally I popped up into blinding daylight. My senses reeled as the light hit me. Before I could take in my surroundings, I felt myself being picked up and propelled towards what looked like a dark moist cavern. I froze as a voice screamed, "Don't put that worm in your mouth!" Too late! I was in that mouth.

Then in a flash a finger quickly scooped me out and a voice said "Nasty nasty, you do not eat worms sweetie," at that I was thrown onto a hard surface. I had barely recovered my breath when, to my horror, a mass of wood sticks was advanced towards me. Soon they entangled me and I was swept over and over again. Wow! That was a close call. I must keep my wits about me. I looked up as the light dimmed, just in time to swerve as a huge foot came crashing down next to me. I know now what Androgynous was trying to tell me. I really shouldn't be up here. I have to go back to down there. Weaving in and out I found myself on soft ground.

"Got you," a delighted voice said. "You're going to catch me a big fish."

Suddenly I felt a sharp pain in my side, and then I found myself dangling on the end of a fishing line. The next minute I was sailing through the air with everything rushing past me. Then, again suddenly, I was in water. I couldn't breathe. Water, water every-where! I tried to hold my breath as I was dunked in and out of the water. At what seemed to be my last breath a disgusted voice said, "This worm's not going to catch anything. I'm changing my bait." Another tearing pain in my side and suddenly I found myself tossed onto some welcoming soft, soft grass.

"Why, why didn't I listen to Androgynous," I moaned to myself. As I slowly started to screw myself downwards I felt myself being picked up; but this time very gently and a voice was saying, "Mummy, Mummy! A lovely worm."

"Yes it is dear, but it looks a little worse for wear. I tell you what. Why don't we bury it? I tucked my tail around me, and then kept very still as I was carefully placed in a hole and covered with earth. I couldn't believe my good luck. Turning myself downwards I continued my journey. Oh my! It felt so good to be in my comfort zone.

As I expected, Androgynous was waiting for me. "Where have you been?" I was asked.

"Nowhere," I whispered, wriggling from side to side.

"If you've not been anywhere then what have you been doing?" Androgynous said.

"Nothing," I said as I looked down.

"You've been up there, haven't you?" was the suspicious reply.

Looking up I answered "Oh I would never go up there," adding to myself, "Never again! No way! This worm had turned!"

Cold Comfort

His watch showed 12:30 pm, November 14th, 1998. After checking his compass, he turned his snowmobile around and began heading southwest. It meant a new route but he was confident it would take him back to the campsite. Slowly he made his way through bush and scrub where the branches encrusted with icicles barely moved. Suddenly he was out on the tundra. There he felt the ice cold winter air begin to whip at his face. Now in the open, he noted how the sun turned the snow into glistening miniature "Stark," he thought, "but beautiful. It really is a wonderful scene!"

"Holy Mother of God!" he screamed to himself, "What was that?" Bringing the snowmobile to a halt he turned it around and slowly began retracing the last 500 feet.

Then he saw it again. A skeleton – propped up in the fork of a stunted tree. With legs propped up at an awkward angle and slack jaw grinning wickedly at him, it looked like some grotesque Hallowe'en display. What had once been hands, clutched a grey package. Stopping, he climbed slowly off the snowmobile and stepped forward to make a closer inspection. Gently he prized off what appeared to be parachute silk from the locked bony fingers. Carefully he unwrapped it to find two scraps of paper inside. Something had been scrawled on them. Examining them more closely he saw each piece was dated. Beginning with the earliest date he read:

"DAY 1. Nov. 14th, 1997. P.M. Around 12.30 pm the plane engine suddenly stopped. I knew immediately I was out of gas. I also knew my only

hope of survival lay in bailing out. Trying not to panic, I fought my way out of the door then, with the wind grabbing at me, I pushed myself away from the falling plane as far as I could.

All I hoped for was that I would land softly and safely on the tundra and that there would be bush nearby where I could shelter from the howling wind. Just my luck!

Instead of the soft forgiving tundra, I hit a grove of small trees breaking both legs in the process.

Day 2. In misery with pain. Trying to take stock of things. During the descent my flying suit gave me some protection. Now propped against a tree and unable to move, I begin to feel the cold creeping in. Suddenly I'm not sure. Will I be rescued in time?

Day 3. Trying hard to retain body heat. Clapping my hands . . . slapping my arms . . . . . rubbing my feet as best I can. Raw cold getting to me. No mercy . . . like water, seeping through. . . gnawing at my bones. Can't feel my feet now. Beautiful day . . .light wind . . . sun shining . . . . icicles on trees and bushes, shining like prisms . . . crazy. Frighteningly beautiful.

Day 4. Now getting dark . . . must stay awake . . . guard against cold . . .

Day 5. Nov. 15th., A.M. Long sleepless night . . . finally daybreak . . . tried moving . . . can't feel feet . . . tried licking snow around mouth . . . tongue began freezing to face . . . finger tips now white . . . waxy . . . hints of blue . . . never felt so cold . . . trouble holding pen . . . Please God let me sleep . . . so cozy . . . please God . . . mustn't sleep . . . got to stay awake so they can rescue me.

Nov. 15th. P.M. No use . . . winter claiming me . . . !"

He could barely make out the signature. Was it Lloyd or Boyd Jamieson? Wiping a tear from his eye, he carefully wrapped the scraps of paper in the remnant of parachute silk and put the package in his jacket pocket. Seated once again on the snowmobile he turned the key. The engine caught, coughed then died. He tried once again. Nothing! Shivering, he knew immediately he was out of gas.

Trilogy

A mighty roar, thrust out with force, tumbling into the unknown.
The journey to the womb is difficult.
A twisting devouring passage, rejection time and time again.
Fighting, pushing, working a path way through the others.
Riding on the backs of the dying, reaching for the destination.
Alone.
Safe.
The glowing circle beckoning.
The red warm chamber inviting.
Conception.

Tick tock, needs are met.
Tick tock we are not there yet.
Tick tock, teenage dreams.
Tick tock, marriage themes.
Tick tock, gurgles , cries.
Tick tock, no more ties.
Tick tock, work force done.
Tick tock, time for fun.
Living.

Time speeds by and once again,
To reassess the now and then.
Peace, strife, laughter, tears.
Tick, tock, where are those years?
Ah yes within the heart — deep sigh.
Until we say the last good bye.
Death? No.
Rebirth!

Volunteers

Reuter: September, 1994.

It's been reported that a recent savage sandstorm which hit a desert area two hundred miles south of Tunisia has revealed the remnants of a war plane.

It was found to be British and from W.W. II. After considerable digging the skeletons of the crew of three were found in the fuselage. It is felt that the plane came down in a severe desert storm and was eventually covered by sand.

Debris was scattered over a wide area. The crew died on impact. Dogtags identified the remains and the next of kin will be duly notified.

* * * * *

September, 1939.

"Come on, tell me! Where've you been," Betty asked her brother.

"Mind your own business," he replied. With that he took off to his bedroom. It wasn't really his bedroom. It was one that he had shared with his two older brothers who were now in the army. Sitting down on the side of the bed he twiddled his cap in his hands – muttering, "When she knows she's going to skin me alive."

Suddenly Betty rudely pushed the door open and yelled, "Come on! You're in some sort of trouble. If you don't spill it I'm telling

Mum." Bert looked up at the angry face of his sister, thought for a moment, then blurted out, "I've joined the Air Force."

"What!" She exclaimed, then grabbing his hand she whispered, "But you won't be eighteen for a couple of more months."

Bert pulled his hand away sharply and kicking one boot against the other replied, "Well it was only a matter of time before my call-up papers arrived."

Looking at him very gently, with her hands twisting around each other, she inquired softly, "What's Mum going to say, Bert? You're her baby."

September, 1939.

Lord and Lady Denby sat quietly together after their customary post-prandial brandy. With its wall-to-ceiling windows covered in dark heavy velvet, it was hardly a cozy room. The unlit fire only added to the chill. Their faces had a look of resignation. Lady Denby, knowing her son, knew there was no changing his mind. His father had forewarned her that Harry would volunteer the moment war was declared. After all Harry was a skilled pilot and God knows there were few of them around. Who would have thought that Sunday afternoon flying would become this? Her only child, born with the proverbial silver spoon in his mouth was now to face all sorts of unknown dangers. Her mind drifted back to the First World War. Wasn't that the war to end all wars? "Damn Hitler!" she thought as she finished off her brandy. At that moment the door opened and there he stood in his pilot officer's uniform with a wide grin on his face. Gone were the grey flannels and jaunty sweater. "Sorry, I joined up ahead of the game," he grinned.

"Just in time for a brandy old chap," his father said to him. Harry spent the next couple of hours bringing them up to date with the war effort, all the while taking great pains to assure his parents he would come through the war with flying colours.

September 1939.

"How could he leave them?" Lilly asked herself as she wiped her hands on her pinny, all the while watching Joe as he played with the children. "He's a good man," she thought to herself. Despite miners being exempt she knew eventually he would join up if the war continued. But why did he have to volunteer? She had always known that Joe hated the pits with the dirt and the hewing coal out of the seams day in and day out. Riding for an hour on his rusty old bike to and from the pit, finishing off with a bath in a metal tub in front of the fire. Yes, Lilly could understand his yearning to get away but she had her yearnings too.

No more wash tubs, no more children, no more boiling kettles over an open fire to fill metal bath tubs. Joe desperately wanted out from the poverty and the air force seemed to be the answer. "Just to fly free in the air instead of being buried in a damp, cramped coal mine," he'd told her. Then taking her face between his hands he'd said, "Look love, this war isn't going to last long, then I'll be home with you and the kiddies and maybe things will be better."

Lilly sighed and smiled knowing that once again he'd won her over.

The War Office, London, W.1. December 1994.

We regret to inform you . . .

MAXINE SLATER-STOCKER

I was born in Vancouver, Canada, educated in country schools in Ontario, girls' school in British Columbia, then Teachers' Colleges at UBC, University of Brock and the College of Art in Toronto. I taught in BC grade schools and Ontario. Married and raised a son and daughter; Ron and I bought into Maple Leaf Golf and Country Club in a fit of wild enthusiasm in April 2003.

We now 'summer' in Courtenay B.C. on Vancouver Island.

3 Five Dollar Deals

December 2008

Scene # 1

A five dollar bill was caught in a bramble hedge. Two children playing hide-and-seek found it and proceeded to fight over it.

"It's mine! I saw it first! I am taking it home to mom."

"No, you don't, its' mine. It is on my side of the street! "

"We'll see who's side of the street it stays on, watch this..."

And with that, the first child balled up the money and threw it up to the sky. The two of them watched as it silently floated through the air, over their heads and down, down, down through the grating to the murky sewer below.

Scene # 2

A rheumy-eyed derelict came slowly down the street. His tattered coat, dirty ripped pants, days old whiskers and pungent odor told of a lifetime failure. When he bent precariously over to tie the strings of his old shoe, he spied a blue piece of paper balled up and stuck into the side of a city park bench.

"Oho, what's this?"

Shakily, he smoothed out the paper and discovered that it was a five dollar bill. Tears formed in the corner of his eyes. He wiped them away with his crusted cuff, coughed a bit, then eased down on the bench to think. As he sat caressing the money, his eyes had a faraway gaze.

At last he rose and retraced his steps back down the block to the corner cafe. He walked slowly but resolutely through the restaurant to the best table in the house, beside a window overlooking a busy street.

"Oh, Tom, you can't stay here now, the manager is in today so I won't be able to get you anything. You must go quickly. "

"That's alright, Missy, I'll have a pot of tea, then you can keep the change of this here fiver."

Scene # 3

The skinny young girl hefted the large bag of newspapers once again onto her bony shoulders. Seventy customers! It was too much, especially on the week-end with feature inserts and all those ads. Mom had been right about it not being a good thing for a girl to do but she had insisted that her two chums had had newspaper routes for over a year – and besides she hated baby-sitting.

Well, she had the last half still to deliver as well as to collect from Mrs. 'Ugly'... Some customers rarely were at home and even when they were, they were miserable. Half the time the girl didn't even bother to collect her money.

She left the monster bag on the bottom step and slowly climbed the stairs with the one paper.

"Well there you are young lady; you look dog tired carrying that big bag, no wonder you forget to come to collect. Here is my overdue payment and a five dollar bonus. Your boss said it was your birthday last week. You better use the money toward purchasing a wagon."

An Almost Widow

January 07, 2012

My friend is an almost widow.
Everywhere she goes –
so goes the coffin.
Empty, of course
but waiting and ready.
The weight / wait of it – heavier than if occupied.
The awareness of it – evident in every thought and deed.
What an awful bulk to bear – this invisible presence.

Silently she screams her pain.
Her soul writhing as Its tendrils are drawn taut –
Dragging the monstrous weight.

Each ribbon of hurt felt with every conflicting thought;
Love of the man that used to be –
Fury at this shell that will not go to – "ITS JUST REWARD".
And GUILT, GUILT, GUILT of these treasonous murmurings.

Death on the Naas

March 2011

The Naas River flows into the Pacific Ocean north of Prince Rupert, British Columbia. Its many tributaries tumble down from the coastal mountains to form a swirling powerful roadway between the natives' villages. The shifting sandbars beneath the waves, as well as submerged logs are always a threat to safe navigation. This river is a test to many skills.

The village in which I was teaching, Kincolith, was on the B.C. coast, the point of land where Alice Arm from the north and the Naas from the east flow into the ocean. The church choir, of which I was a member, had been invited with the other villages along the Naas, to a church dedication ceremony at the village of Ianch, some nautical miles up the river.

We had left our village in a flotilla of three fishing boats, with a dozen or so people to a boat. Our skipper carefully wove around the sandbars and up the river until we came to a landing at a wide bend. We disembarked onto the shore and walked up the little beach to a cluster of river-tossed logs where we stopped and waited... and waited. Nothing here but bush backing up to the mountains.

"What are we doing here, waiting for a bus?" this city girl asked.

"Yes," giggled several people.

Someone built a bonfire and they made tea. I sheepishly shared my bag of peppermints – the only edible thing I had brought (thoughtless city influence). One of the elders said if they didn't hurry up he would be forced to find and kill a porcupine to roast for our meal. He assured me that it was much like chicken. The idea did pique my curiosity, but I didn't get the opportunity to try it because then the 'bus', a beat-up old mail van, came out of the bush to our aid.

What a wild ride! Pelting through the bush over rutted, rocky trails, whizzing past waterfalls, meadows of colourful wildflowers and even over the corner of a lava field, evidence of a volcano some hundred years past. We flashed by astonished bears, smaller furry critters not easily recognized at this speed and some majestic eagles disrupted from their cedar-pole perches. I was given a place of honor on the first tour to exit the landing, squeezed in with several lady-elders and all of the village luggage. Whenever we hit a pot-hole, we would all be airborne, high-fiving the van's roof. My terror of the situation segued into hysterics and I led the group in peals of laughter.

We arrived at a spot across the river from the host village. Long dug-out boats with powerful motors on the stern awaited to ferry us across the rapids on this curving part of the river. I had hoped to go incognito, since my hair at that time was as dark as theirs, wishing to be billeted with a native family. No such luck. I was listed to be roomed with two fusty old school-marms which I quickly declined, opting instead for a cot in the furnace room of the school.

Many events had been planned to make the most of the three day celebration. The natives are excellent sportsmen, keen to show their skills in competition, and so, many events were scheduled for the following day. The choirs were not forgotten either. There was an evening concert of the individual village choirs as well as a few planned songs to be sung together. There were several white teachers attending from the other villages, but I seemed to be the only non-native participating, a fact in which my choir seemed to take great delight.

The following morning on a stroll around the village, accompanied by several friendly children with their dogs, I was comparing my former city's smog to the wonderful aromas of cedar, pine needles, salmon roasting on spits, essences of the river, all wrapped up in the purest breezes blown down from the nearby mountain. What a rush! The church ceremony was a fitting follow-up.

Not long after we had enjoyed our salmon lunch in the town hall and were in the bleachers waiting for the first sporting event to begin, we were surprised to see our elder running out to the field, hailing us with a megaphone.

"Billy Fraser drowned! Billy Fraser has drowned! Billy Fraser has drowned! "He bellowed.

Billy was a sweet, simple boy of fourteen in my grade four class. His family had left him home in our village to look after their grandma. Sadly, he had decided that he was old enough to operate a boat so he had geared up in his heavy work boots and headed up the river, little realizing the treachery of the strong currents and sandbars. The boat overturned and his boots were no match for the river.

Our village quickly assembled, re-crossed the swirling rapids in the power boats to the 'bus' for the somber, jarring ride back to our fishing boats then down the river to home. As soon as I was back, I went to the classroom and removed Billy's desk so that its haunting emptiness would not upset us further. I then gathered up his school books with his art work, looking, as I did so, at the imperfect but hard felt efforts this poor lad had made. I choked back tears, thinking of the sweet spirit in his big awkward frame. I fervently wished that I had been worthy of his good thoughts. I gathered everything and took them, along with a box of tea to his home. Many of the village women were there comforting his mother. After offering my little present, I sat down on a chair near the wood stove.

I did not know what to say. What could I say that would help? The longer I sat looking at the grieving faces and listening to the soft Indian voices, I felt a peaceful comforting and my tears told the mother how I felt even if I could not express it in their language or my own.

On the following morning at school, I instructed each student to write a note to Billy's parents, telling them some happy incident they knew about him. As they were finishing their letters, I looked up the lane to the church and noticed a procession coming down its staircase. The coffin was being carried to a wheeled cart pulled by Billy's family holding onto long ropes. I quickly organized the children into two lines. We ran down a side street and joined onto the ropes with the elders, who were sedately pulling the coffin to a pier at the back of the village. The coffin was loaded onto a boat and taken to their cemetery in a secluded spot up the river. We watched silently as the boat pulled Billy on his last river journey. We returned quietly to class. I think that I read them stories for the rest of the day.

That evening the church bells pealed, calling all to come. The village people were all there to pay homage to the young man. It was a very moving event as everyone took their turn to talk about the boy and how he had affected their lives. Truly, a celebration of a short but meaningful life!

The minister later confided that he was honoured that the villagers had listened to his request that they be progressive on two accounts; they would no longer take the body out of a window, later to be boarded up to keep out evil spirits and they no longer would leave the deceased body wrapped and placed on a high tree branch – but give it a proper earth burial. He was pleased, but I wondered how much of the Native Spirit had been sacrificed for this progress.

Hurricane Charlie

September 2004

What a year this had been. We reveled in the euphoria of our enthusiastic participation in the life of Florida's Maple Leaf Golf and Country Club, otherwise known as 'The Park'. New friends, new thoughts, sunshine, exercise in the outdoors and all those grand things that make a body sing with good health. At the season's end, we experienced a definite let down when we returned to the North. No golf or club activities just around the corner and worse yet, the Arctic winds sweeping over the land blocked any hopes of a pleasant spring. But gradually the weather warmed and we made plans for the gathering of friends at the cottage to ply them with stories of the joys of Florida in 'The Park'.

"Everyone should beg, borrow or steal your inheritance to join this wonderful life style," we said.

Then the world fell apart. Hurricane after hurricane sprang out of the sea, tromping like giants with monster boots, kicking away at our ant hill.

What is broken? What is left? What should we do? The house is ok? The house is a write-off? The house is a wreck? Whom should we believe? So we drove South in the summer heat.

What we saw there was numbing. The pride of ownership which had prevailed in every garden and lanai was shattered. Aluminum strips of roofing were splayed like broken fingers clutching lamp posts; lasagna strips of roofing hung drunkenly down from the car-ports or flopped over bushes; insulation, looking like Kleenex shredded in the laundry, had 'snowed' on everything. Faces of homes were ripped off, exposing the bones of dismantled furniture beneath. Half walls held shelves where books and vases still sat; roof struts had dangling light fixtures blowing in the breeze; blue sky shone through open ceilings; an easy chair facing the TV sat waiting for the master of the house.

Humidity, with over a hundred degrees of heat, sent waves of dew into the air and onto us. Tears and sweat ran in our eyes. Breathing was difficult, your chest hurt. We had to move slowly.

We cleared and swept the piles of effluvia down the driveway and pried giant strips of metal off and dragged then to the curb. Neighbours clutched each other in consolation sharing stories with the tears.

We picked out shards of glass from window frames and surrounding lawn. Hysteria shook us as we unfastened the overgrown vines from plants almost hidden by plastic, insulation and aluminum chunks. Were these the "invasive monster vines" which the garden police had huffily written to us in complaint not two weeks ago? Ahh, the fickle finger of fate!

Hubby inspected the roof and braved its cooking hot surface to patch cuts and small holes. The use of red masking tape added a festive air to the repairs. Even unidentified house chunks were blown up there to start a game of hide-and-seek. Patterns on the surface made by sharp things; branches, windows, a door knob? Even that of a cross marked the kiss of the passing storm.

Most of our trees and bushes survived with just a branch or two missing while one bush, now in bloom, had a necklace of Styrofoam. We commiserated with our next door neighbour whose home had been totally destroyed, yet their Bird of Paradise plant was in full bloom. For a good-bye present?

The memory of endless piles of metal and ersatz juxtaposed with fluttering curtains blowing from a post was so shattering it made us numb. But we could not complain one word as we drove by on our way north, thinking of the poor souls who had had just this one precious place to call home.

Pine Shadows

February 2010

I regret to say that I have a growing resentment to the neighbour's tree – a PINE.

It blocks our morning sun.
It is of course – coniferous. The needles stay ... on.

Unlike the lovely deciduous Maple or Ash who, tho' never asked,
Gracefully drop their leaves like sensuous femmes-fatale
Leaving their delicate lace – like bodies revealed for all the world
to admire
While the pale winter sun shines through their open arms.
Shines through to warm my face and brighten my day.

But the pine grows on – and spreads. Its peak now reaches beyond
my window frame.
This great green bulk with its vigorous growth, shelters many
feathered secrets.
Today it cradles yesterday's snow like a babe – in – arms.

Now I hear the wind begin it's woeful winter song.
Fresh snow halos out around the Pine; boughs shuffle.
Stinging wind comes out of the East, flying toward the house... But,
oh joy –

This great looming oaf – which shades my summer roses
has confounded the winter blow – hard by deflecting its power -
Thus protecting us!

I stand corrected, Pine. You are a friend of mine.
I'll move the roses in the Spring.

Toast and Honey

February 22, 2011

The golden line of honey forms an arc
from Source – to jar – to me.

This golden arc pauses in its pulse of time –
to shine upon its goodness.

To shine – to glow – to emanate
that spirit of goodness from within.

That spirit of all things wonderful
in creatures great and small.

This arc becomes a rainbow
with sweet transformed nectar in its pot.

I can see the flowers in whose being
the golden nectar nestled.

I can smell their fragrance
mingled with the trees, the breeze, the bees.

I'm lying in the cool squeaky grass –
eyes tracing the trail of a bee's travail –
pointing out another succulent flower
to this mighty meandering honey – motor
while he fills his leg – buckets to boast.

Ahhh sweet honey for my toast!

PHYLLIS (SMERAGE) POIRIER

The first 19 years of my life were spent in Hamilton, Massachusetts. I graduated from Hamilton High in 1954 as salutatorian. Beverly Hospital School of Nursing was my next adventure for one year.

I married Robert Poirier in 1955 and we were blessed with four children, 11 grandchildren, six great grandchildren and one great-great grandson.

Treasure Up North

2006

On a picture book day

So sunny and bright

I opened my door

To a startling sight

A sexy black bra

In front of me lay

An unusual sight

To start off my day

Thoughts flashed through my mind

From whence it had come

Erotic, no doubt

Concerning this plum

A young maintenance man

Mowing our lawn

Spotted the garment

I thought it was gone

Was it tossed from the window

Of a hot steamy car

Where uncontrolled passion

Commenced at some bar

Or blown in the breeze

From a balcony rail

Diving and dipping

Like a kite's trailing tail

Cupping his hands to his chest

A smile on his face

He kicked it aside

And continued his pace

It's now been a month

No owners come forth

So I'll show you my treasure

From my summer up north.

My Best Friend

May 30, 1945, my best friend was born. This blond, blue-eyed bundle of joy arrived as my sister.

Janet and I watched the pomp and circumstance of our Memorial Day parade. We stood with my Dad in front of my uncle's gas station in order to be near a phone. Suddenly, he ran out, and grabbed my father. "It's for you, Harold, the baby has arrived." Gingerly, my Dad picked up the phone. He listened for the long-awaited news, and gasped, "Dammit, I'll never get into the bathroom now, it's another girl." That pungent remark will be engraved in my mind forever.

Jealousy permeated my thoughts. I knew my home life would never be the same. I'd surely be the designated baby sitter for years to come. That did not excite me at all. However, it proved to be the best job of my life. If I hadn't been perched on the front steps every day, watching my irritating sibling, I never would have met my wonderful husband. He and his friends drove by quite often, and one day stopped. The rest is history. Time passed, and we all married and went our separate ways. Donna stayed in our hometown, Janet moved many times because of her husband's ministry in the Episcopal Church, and I moved 50 miles away to the other side of Boston.

On many weekends we would spend Sunday at Donna's and grew closer and closer as the years flew by.

After graduating, Donna became a well-known beautician, and an accomplished organist, but something was missing. In her mid-thirties, she decided to become a nurse and follow in the footsteps of our mother. Her great intelligence and compassion proved invaluable to her peers, and she held many top positions. I had tried the same many years earlier, but it wasn't meant to be.

Donna and her family moved to Florida over twenty-five years ago. And I missed her terribly.

We visited yearly, and had wonderful vacations with them. Over the years we've become confidants, and now fate has allowed us to be together again. We lived in Maple Leaf together for six years.

Now she has moved to a new home outside our beautiful park. We don't see each other as much, but I'm proud to say, that my baby sister will always be my extra special friend.

Guess what? She's back!!

Move Over Florence Nightingale: Here I Come!

March 10th, 2005

My mother, Julia, was honored as top nurse in the graduating class of 1931 and I was expected to follow in her footsteps. A nursing career wasn't my life's ambition, but we had no money for college and a three year RN course cost only $150.00. My father won it at the horse races the night before. His passion for the ponies was the reason we were broke. In order to escape parental supervision, I consented to enter Beverly Hospital School of Nursing.

It seemed more like an incarceration rather than freedom. The sparsely furnished, dreary dorm paled in comparison to the large, cheerful, personalized sanctuary I'd left behind. Being assigned to a double room, I encountered 'the room-mate from Hell'. She never showered, brushed her teeth or picked up anything. We used to have surprise room checks and would lose our minuscule privileges if it wasn't perfect. Through the grapevine, I was able to find out the time of these secret invasions and hide her mess under her bed. Some of the real nasty girls would switch the name plate from our door to the most grungy one on our floor. Finally, after much pleading, I was given a private room only to find it infested with cockroaches.

This was my introduction to the hallowed halls of my mother's alma mater.

When we were finally allowed to date, a call would come from the House Mother, "Miss Smerage, you have a gentleman caller."

Since no names were given and I was dating several at a time, it was always a surprise upon entering the musty, antiquated parlor.

The indoctrination period came to an end and I settled into long hours of classes and study. After three months we were placed in a ward and given our first patient. To my delight I drew the men's ward. That excitement didn't last long when I viewed my challenge.

"Hi, Sweetie!" croaked the lecherous ninety-two year old as he pinched my derriere.

The first thing on my orders was to give him a bath. Gasping, I manoeuvred around the tubes protruding from every orifice on his body. What if one came loose and I didn't put it back in the right place? I continued to bathe him gingerly trying not to disturb the maze of rubber keeping him alive. Successfully completing my duty, I started to leave.

"See you tomorrow, honey!" as he again reached for my ample behind.

My next experience was the women's ward. My patient was a very heavy woman with a broken leg. She was supposed to be moved frequently in order to prevent the formation of blood clots. However, she was very stubborn and afraid of pain. She wouldn't budge.

The following day it was my fate to be assigned to the same patient. I apprehensively approached her to begin her morning care. She looked very strange and would not respond.

"Nurse! Nurse!" I shrieked, "Something is wrong with my patient!"

Grudgingly she sauntered over, took one look and callously grumbled, "She's gone. Oh well, I told her to move. Wheel her out and wrap her up, Miss Smerage."

Having never seen a dead person before, let alone touch one, I was frozen to that spot. They put me and the deceased stranger in a small, narrow room near the elevator and closed the door. Trembling with fear, I started to scream. On the other side of the door, everyone was laughing.

"What a baby you are!" they chanted. After what seemed an eternity, a young orderly came to my rescue. He helped me prepare her for the morgue. We rolled her downstairs but she wouldn't fit in the freezer.

"Just leave her here; someone else will take care of it," he blurted and left me there.

"Goodbye! Florence Nightingale, it's all yours! I'm out of here!"

MICHELLE PIFER

I was going to become a Veterinarian or a doctor when I suffered a CVA (Cerebral Vascular Accident) stroke that left me blind and paralyzed.

After months of intense therapy, I was able to overcome the paralysis. However, I remained visually impaired and can see out of my right eye only. My hearing in the right ear was also compromised; I have approximately 15% hearing remaining in that ear. I studied and completed my B.A. in psychology. I became very proficient with the talking computer for the blind.

I share my computer knowledge with others in need. I am always grateful to help people and animals when I can, my faithful seeing-eye companions (Guide dogs) assisting me in these endeavors.

Importance of a Guide Dog

VIP= Visually Impaired Person

A harness on a dog signals that it is WORKING!!!

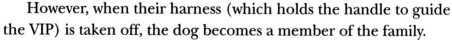

When you are working, there is a time to socialize and a time not to; it is the same with a dog that is performing a job.

You should not pet a dog when it is in harness; this distracts them from their current task!

However, when their harness (which holds the handle to guide the VIP) is taken off, the dog becomes a member of the family.

The dog's transformation is amazing; they know when work is done and play time begins!

Visually impaired people increase their endurance as well as their mobility by causing you to walk faster and with more stability. A VIP gives guide dogs directions such as left, right, forward, find the curb or stairs and even find the building to arrive in many different locations; this gives blind individuals a sense of freedom!

A dog takes you around overhanging branches instead of running you into them and scratching your face. A dog can also take you around objects in the middle of the sidewalk, like holes, children's bike's and toys, bottles, people, etc.

Snow is another obstacle for VIP's. Snow covering slows down a sight-impaired person's movement. A dog will take you on sidewalks that your cane can no longer detect. Thus, snow creates a foreign environment for the visually impaired.

A VIP moves with more ease while indoors because their companion takes them around moving and stationary objects!

When a VIP becomes lost, they must ask for directions. Most people use hand signals or will tell you over here or over there. Dogs usually observe a person's gestures and facial expressions. A dog then gets the blind individual safely and quickly to their designated location. If you tend to be traveling an area you have traveled before, your dog will take over and no directions are necessary.

VIP's who have dogs say that the expense is worth having their independence to move about with ease and direction. The only expense one really has is food. Vet bills are an annual expense and the responsibility of the caring owner. Most VIP's think these expenses are little, in comparison with the cost of feeling helpless in a public place. The relationship is no longer business but a bond of friendship.

A blind individual can travel virtually anywhere with their guide dog, except in an operating room or the ICU (intensive care unit) of a hospital, due to sterilization reasons. When the owner transfers to a regular room in the hospital, their dog can join them.

A dog gives a visually impaired person more self-assurance. They are able to do more for themselves! The only duty a VIP's buddy cannot perform is reading to that person. A dog can be a social benefit as well; more people tend to talk to you when you own a beautiful companion. Dogs, in general, are affectionate and have their own personalities. Each dog has their own way of communicating with their owner to obtain their needs, like bath rooming, feeding and wanting love. Hence, having a best pal is definitely a beneficial part of a visually impaired person's life!

The Time I Nearly Lost My Mind...

I will start this tale by giving you a little history of myself leading up to my blindness. I was a happy little girl who loved animals and people. Later in life I worked with both animals and people, which gave me a wide-variety of jobs, ranging from mucking out stalls to a certified nurse's aide. Then, I enrolled in college. First, I wanted to be a veterinarian because of my work with training dogs and horses. Then I worked with people more and changed my mind. I thought about becoming a doctor or a neurosurgeon, but medical problems began which included headaches, whooshing sounds in my ear and body aches. For months I was seen by a doctor who thought I had no medical problems, that it was psychological because of my age, the fact I was hearing sounds in my ears and my headaches. I wish he would have sent me on to have some tests, but unfortunately this may not have helped. Then a chiropractor diagnosed me with having worms. I took pills for the so-called worms but got no relief. My muscles got so weak I had to quit my job as a nurse's aide because I was afraid I would drop a patient.

One night while I was working as a cashier, I started to hear excruciating sounds in my ears, my head was bursting and I was seeing double. I called my eye doctor the next morning. He was out of town so the receptionist set me up with an appointment to see Dr. Higgins, a Neuro-ophthalmologist, for the next day. After doing a field test and many other vision tests, he realized my optic nerve was swollen. He sent me over to Dr. Jewett's, a neurologist, who sent me to the hospital that very day. While in the hospital, the physician in charge did an echocardiogram, picture of the heart to see how it was functioning. That is when I discovered the sound I was hearing in my right ear was the blood flowing to and from my heart. After that, I had a CT scan and an MRI and was sent home. Five days later, I saw Dr. Fabi at Borgess Hospital and went over the results of the CT scan and the MRI. When I arrived, he looked at me and said "I have some good news and some bad news for you. Which would you like to hear first?" I told him it didn't matter. He

told me that I had to have an operation the next day. If I didn't, I would end up totally blind or dead. He gave me a hug and patted me on the back; I knew everything would be fine. He had discovered an Arterial

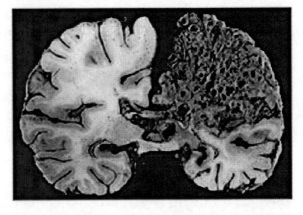

Venus Malformation (A.V.M). A.V.M's usually are not found until you are in your late fifties or early sixties, just my luck. Little did I know that many surgeries were to come?

The main surgery was a craniotomy. Unfortunately, this surgery caused me to have a massive cerebral blood haemorrhage which caused a cerebral vascular accident (stroke) to occur. A portion of my left temporal lobe containing my speech and language center was also removed. When entering my brain, the surgeon also discovered an aneurysm in a crucial state. The stroke left me with temporary paralysis and total blindness. The deficits I am left with are visual impairment, hearing loss of 85% in my right ear, a little ataxia (a loss of muscle control), which is mostly unnoticeable, seizures, and a plastic plate on the right side of my head.

In conclusion, I have overcome many hurdles to be here and am proud of my accomplishments. For example, I have learned to walk, talk and do the basics of everyday life, but that is another story.

MY Epiphany

"Ouch! What is going on?"

My head is full of air,

Like an over inflated beach ball.

The pressure is too GREAT!

Whew, all the tension leaves.

Light an extremely weightless,

I hover looking at the scene below.

"Who is lying on that metal table?

It's ME!"

I stare in disbelief.

Gliding closer, I press my lips tight.

"Jeezy Petes," I stammer.

Beginning to shake, I yell

"Trouble,"

"Trouble,"

"What's wrong with me?"

Floating even closer,

I see

People in white and blue,

Frantically running about,

Their face masks pushed up

My head is open,

"Horrific," I garble!

My doctor is near.

Instruments fly into his hands, like magic!

"Where is my skull?" I scream!

Gasping, I drift away.

"This can't be my surgery," I wail!

"Something definitely is not right."

Oozing blood is everywhere!

"NO," I babble!

"Help me, JESUS",

I bellow and plead!

Gently, I am drawn into a mysterious, but comforting place.

Playing softly and hypnotically,

Seeping into my soul,

Many Musical instruments can be heard…

Birds are canorously   singing, almost inaudibly…

Flitting butterfly like objects surround me…

Many unknown colors engulf me

I am in a magnificent space.

So vast…. words cannot describe it.

However, I feel enclosed and safe!

A voice rings out boisterously,

"Your moment may be near."

Gently touching my shoulder,

A tall, angelic person arouses me,

Giving off tranquility,

An Aura surrounds him

He is so bright!

I feel purified while my whole being fills with peace!

His shimmering, long, lustrous hair,

Sways about his face obscuring his features,

His hands are together as if in prayer,

His enormous feet are encased in plain leather sandals.

They seem to be standing alone.

His presence Portrays gentleness and strength.

"Speaking softly, I ask "Was that your voice?" "

Yes, he smiles and nods!

"Are you ready to go back?"

"No, I want to stay"," I softly murmur

"He replied, No, it is not your time," "

"Time for what, I don't understand?" I ponder.

Understanding dawns!

However, I still wish to remain…

"Hear the people praying for you"

He states and raises his hands.

I see images and mumblings of many.

The tears upon many faces, give me a jolt!

Affecting me most is the sight of my mother and father.

"Come with me and be with your family,"

He firmly states!

"JESUS?" I ask meekly.

For my being knows.

"Yes, now walk with me!"

He staunchly says grasping my hand,

I freeze and begin to weep

He touches my soul!

The feeling was so wonderful,

I did not know what to do,

"No, do not cry, walk with me."

He states this so tenderly and matter of fact that I begin to move.

He smiles down at me!

Harmony and joy

Envelope my whole being

I do not want to leave.

We walk hand in hand.

I feel like a little girl that has lost her way.

Smiling, I keep gazing up.

I think to myself,

"Days must surely, have passed,"

Seeing a bluish white light, I point.

My finger trembles, as I look up.

He says "yes!"

I Implore,

"Not Yet?"

"You must, for your time is running short."

"Be strong my little one" he decisively speaks!!!

Hugging we part,

With a love, I will never forget.

I am above my body again.

I see the doctor using a heart thumper

There is a bag of blood hanging on an I.V. pole.

Next thing I know

I am

BACK...

I will never be the same!

My Jesus,

My Jesus,

Miracles do happen!

JOHN WRIGHT

For John, English was always a gratifying subject in that he enjoyed writing while at school. Later, his pleasure in the English language was to serve him well in business, and later, in writing skits for his retirement community's (Maple Leaf) annual variety show.

No Picnic

L ooking up from the letter I'd brought home from school the previous day, my father announced, "You're going on a school picnic – today." Even as he was saying this I couldn't help noticing that, while he had spoken to me, he hadn't taken his eyes off my mother standing quietly behind me.

"Today?" I yelped, turning to look up at my mother. Smiling softly she nodded but said nothing as she turned to lay out my things for school. "Whoopee!" I yelled. "A picnic!" This memory took place in Edinburgh, Scotland. At the time I was six years of age. It was a Friday and school had just returned from summer holidays that week. The date – September 1, 1939.

The only thing different in my mother's laying out my school things that morning was a bag of goodies she was also assembling. Sandwiches make sense at a picnic of course, however, "What do I want with toothpaste and underwear on a picnic?" I asked her as she pinned a label, with my name on it, to my jacket.

"Oh you never know," she smiled, strangely quiet. "You may have to stay overnight." The other thing different that morning was my father's goodbye. Always a kind and gentle man for sure, but not given to lingering and hanging on – as I felt he did that morning.

It was as if he didn't want to let me go.

That morning school was a seething mass of excitement. *"With good reason!"* I thought to myself. *"It's not every day the whole school goes on a picnic."* Even the teacher, new to us that week, was excited. She kept opening the classroom door to check on what was happening out in the hall. Obviously she was waiting for a signal of some sort. Suddenly a bell started to ring urgently. Immediately she lined us up, complete with the gas-masks we had received two or three months earlier. That morning had been the first time our parents had insisted we carry them with us to school. The letter from the school had obviously instructed our parents to make sure we took them with us that day. The teacher marched us out to the playground and assembled us facing the school along with all the other classes. To add to the noise and excitement there was also the throng of parents and other relatives lining the school railings behind us, waving and shouting names. Obviously this was to be some picnic.

Within a moment or two I heard my mother calling my name from somewhere in the crowd. Turning I spotted her laughing and smiling at me all the while gesturing wildly. To re-assure her, I held her bag of picnic goodies up high so she could see I hadn't left it behind in the classroom. Again I found myself wondering, *"Whoever heard of an overnight picnic?"*

The other thing I wondered about was why several mothers appeared to be crying. Soon, under the guidance of our teachers, we were marched out of the school and through the local shopping area to the nearby railway station. Courtesy of the local 'bobbies', there was no traffic on those four blocks that morning – only hundreds of mums and dads walking beside us. Obviously us kids going on a school picnic was important stuff. Many years later I was to learn that throughout the British Isles, over 870,000 school children made a similar journey that day.

Finally we were lined up on the open railway platform which passed beneath the main street. There we waited in a great state of excitement for the train that was to take us to wherever the picnic was being held. All the while keeping us entertained were the parents on the road-bridge above us, yelling down all sorts of encouragement and last minute advice.

I remember thinking that some of the advice I heard didn't fit with what I thought a picnic was all about: "Dinny forget to use yer hankie." "Eat yer porridge!" "Do yer homework!" "Behave yersel!"

I don't remember the actual train trip. All I do remember is everyone getting off at some country station an hour or two later and being walked to a village nearby. Moments later we were lined up in some small hall where local people were already assembled waiting for us. In time one of them, a not unkind looking older-than-my-mum lady, took me to one side and while unpinning my name label on my jacket, gently said, "You're coming with me."

"*Good!*" I thought. "*Now we can get on with the picnic!*"

In time I was to learn we had arrived at the village of Denholm, nestled safely in the Cheviot Hills in the Scottish Borders between the textile towns of Hawick and Jedburgh. Even at the tender age of six I appreciated Denholm to be an extremely attractive village built around a four-sided village green – complete with monument in the centre to some local worthy. Many years later I was to learn that Denholm was a "planned" village as opposed to the normal situation

where a village was simply a small settlement which had grown piece by piece over the centuries. As the result of being a planned village Denholm had one significant building on each of the four sides: a church, a school, a village store and a pub – close by what was to become my home for the next little while. (Photos from http://www. denholmvillage.co.uk/)

Our hosts were the Olivers, to me, a gentle old couple – possibly in their late fifties to early sixties. He was the village cobbler. They had no children and the precipitate arrival of two six year old "townies" in their midst must have been a major upset for them. However, no matter how much angst they may have shared between them, it remained their secret.

My fellow townie was Alan. I'd never met him before but we got along really well and did everything together.

Despite the failure of any picnic to materialize, I settled into the Denholm/Oliver world fairly easily. There was so much new stuff to explore! The house comprised three small floors. The ground floor was Mr. Oliver's tiny shop. We lived on the second floor and slept on the third. We arrived on Friday, September 1st. The following day, Saturday, was devoted to settling us in to our living quarters then in the afternoon being given a tour of Mr. Oliver's shop. In the process of demonstrating how to sole and heel a shoe Mr. Oliver gently established who would be in charge during our stay there. What six year old idiot was going to create a problem for any man who spent his life working with the sharpest knives Alan and I had ever set eyes on?

Sunday September 3rd was the day whose importance I came to appreciate more and more as events unfolded over the next five years. Apparently the Sunday papers were full of something Mr. and Mrs. Oliver found very upsetting. Finally Mr. Oliver looked up from his paper and gravely announced, "There's a war on. (pause) But it's very far away."

"O.K.," I remember thinking to myself. "That's that! There's a war on but Mr. Oliver says it's very far away so let's get on with the picnic – or whatever is supposed to be happening."

One of the first things I had to get used to was not being the only six year old in the world. Having no brothers or sisters I had apparently been very spoiled, though I can't say I had noticed it. At one point in the first week or two Mrs. Oliver announced to Alan and I that Mr. Oliver had a surprise for us and would be coming up from his shop in a moment to share this surprise with us. Quickly I ran through the usual guesses I would make at such moments: new bike, new train set, new this, new that. Finally after checking that we were in place at the head of the stairs he came up with his hands behind his back. *"Can't be a very big bike or train set,"* I thought to myself.

"Shut your eyes," Mrs. Oliver commanded – sounding very excited. Once satisfied our eyes were completely closed she told her husband to hold out his hands. He must have held them out because one second later she commanded us – in triumph – to open our eyes.

We did! In each eye he had a twinkle. In each hand he had a pear. A pear! Not a bike! Not a train set! Just a pear! In my confusion I sensed something important to me had just happened.

However it was to be several years before I got the message that Mr. Oliver's lovely thought was what mattered.

Within days of our arrival in Denholm, school came into our lives once again. Every classroom of the local school was suddenly crowded to overflowing with both the pre-existing village kids and us new 'townies'. Luckily we all got along just fine. As for supplies, our teacher simply made the five hour round trip to Edinburgh by bus on the weekends and brought back all she could carry for the Monday morning. The other reason why any further thoughts of a picnic began to disappear was the new forms of entertainment that came from living in the country – as opposed to living in the city.

Denholm offered us townies three new sources of entertainment. The first was "conkers" of which few of us had any experience. Conkers was the name given to threading three or four chestnuts on to a piece of string roughly 14 to 15 inches in length. That done, you simply challenged anyone else walking around with a similar string in their hand. As the challenger you held out your string of conkers with the bottom chestnut dangling on its own because you had the other chestnuts safely in your hand – but still threaded on the string.

Your opponent would then take a swing at your conker trying to smash it to smithereens with his bottom conker. He was allowed only one swing. If he failed to destroy your conker then it was his turn to hold up his string and let you have a go. September was chestnut time and the village green boasted two or three magnificent horse-chestnut trees. Alan and I were shown how to bring down the green clad chestnuts by throwing sticks or broken branches at them. Occasionally one of the bigger boys would help us. Stripping away the outer green protective pith revealed the beautiful rich conkers beneath. We would then take these to Mr. Oliver to string for us. After all, he had all the right tools to do the job.

Despite his bemusement when, during the school lunch hour, we took our first batch of shiny new chestnuts to him, he told us our strings would be waiting for us after school that day. Sure enough when we rushed home that afternoon there they were – to our eyes, the best strung conkers in all of Scotland!

A second form of entertainment we cottoned on to very quickly was round-up time. Round-up came about when some local farmer, for whatever reason, and usually about lunch time, would herd a few cows through the village. In they would come at the eastern end of the main street, and out at the western end. Total length of street – roughly 500 yards. No problem. That is, no problem until the lead cows drew level with the open entrance to the village green. Immediately they spotted the richest and most beautiful grass known to the bovine world, they would charge through the gates and on to the green. Even with both the farmer and a farmhand yelling all sorts of things they were unable to prevent the stampede. However, help was always close at hand – provided it was school lunchtime. Most of the time it was. Nowadays I suspect the farmer chose lunchtime to herd his cows through the village. That way he could depend upon the school kids to herd the cows off the green.

The first time we townies saw the cows break away from their herders and charge onto the village green it was lunch-time. Immediately the school playground, immediately next to the village green, emptied of village kids for they knew what was about to happen. Naturally we townies followed them.

First the young villagers circled the cattle, and then when everyone was in place, they started to yell and flail their arms while closing in on the cows. Most of us townies didn't know cows prefer to keep their distance from humans. Impressed, we watched our horse-less cowboy kids move the herd back through the gateway and out on to the street again. Naturally the next time there was a stampede we big city kids joined in and with great enthusiasm restored law and order to Denholm. After that, round-up became a highly anticipated event.

A third form of entertainment was introduced by the local minister who invited all the kids (village and town) to church one Saturday morning and, for our entertainment, put on a lantern slide show! I was delighted of course, but it seems every city kid but me had been in the habit of going to Saturday matinee where Flash Gordon was the big attraction.

For them a lantern slide show was way out of date but I was charmed by the idea and, together with the village kids, was totally captivated.

Despite the shortness of my stay (3 months) and the length of time since it happened (73 years) there is no question my evacuee's visit to Denholm left me with many warm and wonderful memories: the charm and beauty of the village and surrounding countryside, the warmth of the people who suddenly had all those children thrust upon them and told to make the best of it, in turn the country experiences thrust in upon city kids. There is no question I am a better person for the experience – and, to this day, a happier one.

Meanwhile, because he had served ten years in the Cameron Highlanders, my father had been recalled to military service immediately war broke out. That left my mother completely on her own. Naturally she wanted to see how her only child was faring in Denholm. That meant a one-day visit by bus. Everything went well – except for one thing! The Wrights' Edinburgh house was at that time a modern one (built 1936) and lit by electricity whereas the Olivers' Denholm house, possibly over two hundred years old, was lit by oil lamps. Those lamps terrified my mother. All she could think of was one of them being knocked over and the house being burned to the ground. Finally, with the Phoney War (September 1939 to May 1940) settling into place, she insisted with the Edinburgh School Board that I be allowed to return home with the understanding she and I would move out of the big city and join my father in the small Scottish town to which he had been posted.

Before my big day of travelling all on my own on a bus back to Edinburgh, with label bearing name and address once again pinned to my jacket, I had a brief but significant exchange with another boy. Compared to my six years he was at least eight or nine and therefore much more knowledgeable. While we were idly standing on the corner of the main street an army dispatch rider roared past us on a motorbike, making lots of noise in the process. I asked the other boy what the dispatch rider was up to. He looked at me and started to laugh. "Silly bugger!" he said, "Dye' no ken there's a war on! What d'ye think yer on? A school picnic?"

CHRIS VAUGHAN
*Chris was born Christine Cannell in Los Angeles, California in 1939.
Moved to Canada as a teenager and then met and married George
Vaughan in l960. Currently residing in Guelph, Ontario during the
months of April to October and Port Charlotte, Florida for the winter
months.*

A Lament to the Speeding Golf Carts

Or

What in the Hell is the Matter with You Guys [Girls]?

Speeding down Scotia comes a golf cart— full out

Two wheel right turn from the left lane, tipping— just about.

Thought I recognized him, his golf cart's painted red

But couldn't quite be sure of that 'cuz "darn!" away he sped.

Heard the neighbours talking, I couldn't help but overhear

About the crazy golf cart guy who nearly put them on their ear.

"Was his golf cart red?" I asked. They said, "No, it was bright blue."

Ah, another golf cart guy with a cart of a different hue.

Now I'm coming home from shopping and I'm signalling my turn

Then I check the rearview mirror and I really start to burn!

My signal says I'm turning right and there's a golf cart guy

He's passing me, but on the right! I try to catch his eye

Then brake and turn to watch him as he comes up my right side

He smirks at me, then turns his head and continues on his ride.

His cart was kinda spiffy, with an awning white and green

and I realized that this was a cart I'd never seen.

So here was yet another of those crazy golf cart guys

Who really need to take control and learn how they should drive.

They lose their freaking marbles when they get behind the wheel

I'd like to catch just one of them and ask "What is the deal?'

I hear a screech, a high pitched giggle and look up to see a cart

She came right through the stop street, I almost missed that part!

Then she wheeled around the landscape lady, lost direction, near upended

And quickly turned the cart away and didn't stop for one half second.

Her cart was brown, with a couple of flags and a teddy bear in the back seat

She's on her way to somewhere and, by gosh, she won't be beat!

It seems to be the rule for golf cart guys when they are out to play

Ignore the stop streets, ignore the signals and take the right of way

You can pass on the right, pass on the left and drink as well as drive

And so I ask with much respect "What the Hell is the matter with you guys/girls?"

December 22/11

International Travel with a Costco Card

[tongue in cheek]

November 17/11

L ast year I learned that you can travel with a Costco card. At 72 years old, I thought I had seen everything but this was something new.

We were going on a cruise and as part of the deal we were to be treated to a tour of the *state of the art* new ship on which we would be cruising. We arrived at the port authority with homeland security in full important swing when I realized I had forgotten my purse at home. Home was a four hour drive. So no photo ID and no time!

"Oh well!" our travel agent Suzanne said, "this is only a tour and the captain can arrange for you to tour the ship without the photo ID. After all, we aren't even leaving the port!" Our group began to file through security and gather on the other side of the dividing wall. Suzanne was frantically trying to reach the captain of the ship who was taking a nap and couldn't be reached. The head security man was eyeing me with suspicion. I must have looked very dangerous because he kept shaking his head and looking at me every few minutes. I was standing against a wall while the group was filing past me. He was, apparently, a very important person in the security line-up business.

There was a gentleman who was in almost the same predicament as I was, but he had a Costco card with his picture on it. He may have obtained it in Canada just after he arrived from the outer reaches of Somalia where he had been taking flight training, who knows? But—he had a Costco card. With his picture on it! So, voila! Photo ID. And "Yessir! Right this way!" My sister went to the Bahamas with nothing but a Costco card. Go figure.

So, believe it! You can travel with a Costco card. It has your photo on it and, therefore, is acceptable. Doesn't matter whether you have subversive intent – that card is your ticket to travel. The security guard may turn your card over to see what is on the back, turn it back over, study it, raise his eyebrows, mutter to his co-workers and query you "What is this?" But when you reply that it is your Costco card, all is well and he will wave you on. Trust me!

Now, another question is "Would a Sam's card do just as well?" How about a Maple Leaf Estates card or just a student ID card? Does it have to be a Costco card? And, can you be smiling on that card. If so, then I would prefer that to my passport which has an unsmiling face that really bears no resemblance to the real me. I have a happy and cheerful face. My passport picture depicts me as if I had just lost seven family members in a plague epidemic that has devastated the nation and left me the sole survivor. It bears absolutely no resemblance to the person that I see in the mirror every morning and so, I fail to see that it is an accurate identification of me. A Costco card would work better for me.

Our very embarrassed Suzanne finally gave up her quest to find the Captain and loaded my husband and me into a taxi. We went to the beach to a very nice restaurant, with wine. We had a lovely lunch while our group toured the ship and had their lunch in the *state of the art* dining room.

Suzanne made a note to suggest to future travelers that they carry a Costco card at all times and I made a note to apply for one as soon as I returned to Canada.

Alan's Prayer

Okay, Alan, now comes the hard part
When I have to deal with the ache in my heart.
When every day I want to ask how you are?
But you are not here, you have gone so far.
It seems that you might give me a sign
That you are looking down and that you are fine.
If I only knew that this was true
It would give me peace, remembering you!
A world without you is lacking for me
And there's a space where a blue eyed boy should be.
So I'm going to fill it with every memory
And trust that you know you are still here with me.

Lovingly composed for Alan's family and friends

Plea Bargain

I am teen — betwixt and between!

Shall I follow your rules?

Every day, go to school?

Act appropriately?

Then this is my plea!

Will you give me the chance — to dance?

Will you let me try — to fly?

Let me grow?

Let me know — I am teen!

Fear [a Mom's reply]

I am Mom — conflicted and scared!

That you won't go to school,

That you'll break all the rules!

And this is my fear —

That I can't keep you near!

When you engage in the dance — will you take that last chance?

If you try to fly — could it be too high?

Can I let you go?

I don't know — I am Mom!"

January 19, 2011

Canadian Cowboy

Arriving at the coliseum grounds with my show horses, I backed the horse trailer into a temporary parking spot near the doors leading into the barn area and made my way inside to the show secretary's office. I needed to get my stall numbers so that I could unload the two horses I had brought to show in the halter classes the next morning. My classes were first thing and my entries had been made by mail. I would be out of here by noon the next day but maybe I could take some time this afternoon to watch some of the reining classes that were going on. I could hear on the announcements that they were performing now and this was always a favourite class of mine. It showed the horse at its athletic best. What I did in the halter arena was showing form to function. Breeder's were doing it right if the horses that won in the halter class went on as adult horses to win in the performance arena.

I got my stall allocations and returned to the parking lot to unload the horses and get them settled for the night. Both box stalls were clean and bedded with straw and conveniently there was an empty standing stall next to them. The show secretary had said I could use that stall for my equipment as no one else had purchased it. There wasn't too much equipment for two halter classes. Just my silver show halters, leather leads and the dusting and polishing stuff for the horses themselves. I used baby oil and rags mostly along with the usual curry combs and brushes. Some hoof treatment stuff and a can of Show Sheen finished up the paraphernalia. The point of the halter class was to show the horse on the lead line bare of any tack but the halter and lead and the judge decides if your horse has the conformation needed to perform the activities that will be required of him as an adult animal. That's basically it and if the judges are honest and put the best horse first then the breeding programmes will produce the best horses. Doesn't always work that way but that's the idea. I was going to show a yearling filly and a weanling colt, both products of our own breeding programme and sired by our own stallion. We had high hopes for these two but then we were competing against some others who had the same high hopes. Tomorrow would tell. I got my horses settled, watered and fed. I checked my tack to make sure I had everything I would need in the morning and then headed off to the coliseum to watch some reining.

I got to the ring in the coliseum, walking through the exercise area where the horses await their turn to compete, and stood at the rail. A cowboy was just finishing his event. This is a singular event in which each competitor rides a pattern previously designated by the judges. Patterns are numbered and the competitor should know each one by the number. When he enters the arena he knows what pattern he must run for the judges. The next entrant was coming into the ring and I caught my breath when I saw the horse begin his pattern. Gallop to the centre of the ring and slide, very long with haunches tucked underneath, while front hooves daintily stepped quickly forward in front of the slide. Nice back up, about fifteen feet and straight. Beautifully done! The horse was something special. Golden palomino, with long flaxen mane and tail! The tail was long and flowing and nearly dragged the ground, the mane hid a slender arched neck upon which perched a beautiful sculptured head with small alert ears pricked forward. He had big brown eyes widely spaced which made me think he probably had some smarts. The cowboy continued his ride with two spins, four to the right and four and a quarter to the left. It looked like he was trying to screw one hind foot after another into the ground. Now the rider began the circles required with Pattern #10 and ended with the two rollbacks and another beautiful slide. He hesitated indicating to the judges that he had completed his pattern. There was lots of applause for this ride.

The cowboy dismounted and taking one rein, the other flung over the saddle, walked toward the judge, head humbly bent, looking at the ground. Stepping up to the judge, he reached up and taking the top of the bridle in his hand pulled it over the horse's ears and dropped the bridle for the judge as was required. The judge gave him a nod and he exited the ring, stopping just outside, he undid the waist buckle of his chaps and bent over to unzip the sides. Removing them he hooked the chaps over the saddle horn. He was tall with a beautifully shaped hat, no strings and whistles for this boy, and his belt buckle denoted some success in the arena. It was silver, engraved with something I couldn't read without looking too interested, and his spurs were silver as well, jingling, as he moved around his horse loosening the girth and making sure the horse was comfortable.

I was standing right there and couldn't resist a comment. "That was a really nice ride, cowboy! Your horse is terrific isn't he?"

I expected a "Yup" or "Thanks" or even just a nod with a finger to the hat brim but I heard "Oui, merci!" and realized that this Canadian cowboy was a francophone and as good a cowboy as I had ever seen. He likely hailed from the Province of Quebec in Canada and riding reining horses was his hobby.

GENA SHIBLEY

Gena was born in Ontario but lived much of her life in Michigan. Her husband Jack was in the military and they spent years abroad in Hawaii, the Philippines and Iceland. During those years she taught kindergarten, the learning disabled and the emotionally impaired. After receiving her Masters of Education in Administration, she finished her teaching career in the Upper Peninsula of Michigan. An accomplished pianist, she now divides her time between Florida and Ontario.

Procrastination

March 5th, 2009

Procrastination is a topic I've been trying to write about for ten days...or should that be... for about ten days I've been trying to write about procrastination??? Hmmm! You might realize – if you think about it – I've had nothing to offer this writing class for nigh on the last two times we've met. Several of the excuses I've given over that period of time have been redundant: too many guests, too little sleep, too much food.... However, it's going on the second week since various ganglia (ganglion is singular) of our family have departed, so it is time to settle down... (should I define ganglia??) (to do so might be construed as redundant... but not to do so might lead, inadvertently, to confusion)... I will think about this.

I noticed in the first sentence I wrote, inadvertently, objectional grammar. To wit, the object of the preposition 'about' should probably be the adverbial phrase 'for ten days'- thus answering 'how long'... but then I don't really need that dangling preposition and could omit it. I'll get around to changing it when I edit this paper.

To return to the present problem of procrastination I will return in a moment. I have been sidetracked by prepositional phrases. I'm sure you know what I mean.

To procrastinate is to tarry unnecessarily, (that word looks wrong, but) implying a hint of denial and perhaps reluctance to continue and/or to reinforce one's motivation. (Should one use 'one'?) That last word in the previous sentence, 'motivation' is derived from the old Latin word (actually all Latin words are old but then, so are most words if you really think about it)... the old Latin word, *moveo – ere-ovi- otum*, meaning to move, or shift...but I digress.

I'm very thirsty. I must make some tea. I could (would? should?) postulate (like that word!) that one can think far more clearly after imbibing in (do I need the word in?) the caffeine and tannic acid of *Lipton's* tea. Of course, there are those who would prefer *Tetley's* in a heartbeat. Either one, if steeped properly, can contribute to the art of *eastern meditation* (do I need italics and should that have been capitalized, or not???) as opposed to the somnolence (LOVE that word) of *western prayer* (same question). Columbian coffee is far too stimulating for either (but some may disagree).

I must get back on track after wandering?... delaying? ... getting off topic... YES!... wandering afar from the subject of procrastination...it's easy to think of something else.

Ahem... It is easy... simple... no! ... easy ... to get started about writing on a topic such as that of procrastination. The concept concerns us all (perhaps some more than others) – and should that be in italics or not...

Oh well! It is very difficult to stick to something to completion (could I put that a better way) without putting it off. (never end a sentence with a preposition... must edit this tonight at the latest!)

There are many interruptions, both the cerebral (lofty, brainy) as well as the sensorial (sensory, auditory, tactile, corporeal... hmm) kinds. I'll have to check that parallel construction before

I'm finished with this fragment of thought (but it will have to be done later).

I just glanced at the clock and it's time to practice my arpeggios (should I define this… these…those???) I can't risk the deterioration of flexibility in my right wrist by gripping my pen any longer…. So, I will definitely finish this piece of writing tomorrow. Wasn't Annie a great show???

604 words & will jj kill me for going over by 104 – must edit – SOON!!!!

White Out

January 2009

Dialogue/Fiction

The man and woman in the tan van sped northward over the rolling hills. The two-lane highway was a narrow asphalt strip; white solid lines on either side defined the tasseled grasses that grew into the deep ditches. The driver, a lady of middling years glanced at the wan, whiskered face of the man slumped beside her. His seat harness strained to push his shoulder securely to the seat back.

"He looks so weak," she mused. Aloud she spoke softly, "We'll be home soon. I made some fresh soup with lots of beef and noodles in it. The protein will give you some energy."

He glanced at her, and with a half-smile shook his head, "I just want to get in that door and crawl into bed."

She nodded and increased her speed. A white car passed them. Its red taillights faded toward the hill, waiting in the distance. The road ahead was clear. As she glanced at the autumn landscape around her, she watched the late afternoon sun spreading yellow stains across the rocky pastureland. The leaves burned as crimson as the car's taillights still receding in front of her.

"Such a perfect afternoon!" she sighed with relief. She glanced at her husband tenderly. His eyes were closed, his shoulders drooping. Soon they would be home. The coming weeks would be filled with hope and healing. She leaned back in her seat and began to concentrate on the road ahead of her.

She jerked her head. Those taillights seemed closer than before. Too late, she realized the white car with the round, red rear lights was not moving. The orange, left-turn signal flashed into her sight, the rhythmic pulse making it very plain there was no time to stop.

"I'll get around it." Decision made, rejected, made again.

She wheeled to the right. A wrenching grind screeched long beside her. The engine lunged into the white fender. The van rocked upward, then tipped backward into the deep culvert.

"So this is what it's like to die."

Gradually all motion ceased. The silence screamed at her. All her senses were alive. She saw the white cloud envelope her, smelled the sweet oil. She glimpsed the bright light in front of her and heard the soft minor ripple of sound reaching into her head. She tasted liquid warmth between her teeth.

"How slow it is," she wondered.

The voices swarmed louder and louder. Then… there was shouting.

"Turn off your key!"

"Turn off your key, *NOW*!"

"Hold it down!"

"Steady… steady…"

Her head pushed down into something hard. Darkness surrounded her. A slice of air shivered over her face as her head tipped to the left.

"Ease it open… real slow."

"She'll tip!"

"Careful, the glass there!"

"Did she get the key out?"

Light drifted in, slicing her right cheek.

"My God; is he…?"

"He's okay. That blood is from cuts."

"Careful; ease him out."

"Lucky that harness held … *CAREFUL!*"

Gradually, as she was pulled sideways, the woman tried to open her eyes. She squinted under a swollen eyelid. The cold air reached the back of her neck.

Then she knew.

The white air bag was being pulled from her face. It lifted up from her body. The light from the fire truck, the siren still wailing, shone through the shattered windshield in a kaleidoscope of twisting shapes.

"They're both alive – *all right!*"

"Lucky people…"

"They're both lucky people."

"*Thank you!*" I whispered as I leaned against the opening door.

"Out of the Mouths of Babes..."

January 2009   "Ghost" Story

I met my daughter before she was born. That's pretty hard to wrap your thoughts around, but it's true. It happened like this.

My husband and I had been married for five years before our son was born. We were posted to Langley Air Base in Hampton, Virginia. We bought a house. I taught second grade in Phoebus, on the 'wrong side of the tracks!' The state school had just been integrated that fall. Teaching dynamics were changing; supplies were few, schoolrooms shabby, parents divided, teachers wary and the kids were scared. Days were busy. Life was full of love and challenge.

Our son, Angus, grew bright and bonny. He loved books, sideways and upside down. As I read to him each night, he gradually began to "read" them himself. After the nightly read and the light turned off, he would wait until he was alone. Then he'd turn on the light and read his books again.

His father worked until midnight and, exhausted from my day, I made a momentous decision. "Okay, Angus; here's your milk and peanut butter. Choose the ten books you want and when you're finished, turn off your light. Good-night, dear."

"'Night Mum," he grinned with satisfaction. I closed his door and walked across the hall to our bedroom. This continued for several nights and we were both satisfied with the new arrangement.

One night, several weeks later, I had barely sunk into sleep when I was startled awake by giggling and whispering. I listened for a few minutes. All became quiet so I went back to sleep. The next night, the same thing happened. This time, I decided to get up to check on my son.

I tiptoed to his door and again heard great merriment and loud whispers, punctuated by short pauses. I peered in the keyhole. The streetlight shone on Angus' hand. He gripped a wooden block, holding it high above his head. He listened; then he pulled it back to his mouth. He whispered into the 'microphone'; then he stretched out his arm, pointing it into the space toward the ceiling. He looked and listened intently, then gurgled with laughter so heartily that the pillowcase beside his head was wet with spit. This performance was repeated several times. I could not wait to find what was going on and why. As I opened the door, I saw his books, still stacked on the bedside table, but the milk and sandwich were gone.

"What up, Angus?"

"Jest talkin', Mom," he answered.

"Who are you talking to?"

"Oh," he beamed, "I'm talkin' to my baby sister."

"Say that again?"

"I'm talkin' to my sister and she's talkin' to me," he chuckled.

"But Angus, you have no sister."

"I know, but I'm gonna' get one," he replied matter-of-factly. "She says she's coming to live with us."

"And when might she be going to do that?" I asked rather dryly.

"Oh, next year sometime, when she's ready," Angus yawned.

"That's really interesting, Angus. It *is* getting late. Tell her goodnight and go to sleep." I gave him a kiss, patted his head and looked around carefully as I closed the door.

For the next few months, this new behavior became the routine. My husband and I laughed at our son's active imagination and wondered how normal it was and how long it could last. We were content with our life as it was, no changes were desired.

I *did* become pregnant. We gradually included our son in the family plans and expectations. The nocturnal conversations still continued from time to time. We became used to the bursts of laughter behind the bedroom door. This was a time before ultrasound and we were concerned that a boy might join our family.

A few weeks later we woke up suddenly. We listened. There was silence – no chattering – no giggles. It was the same the following night.

In the morning, as I prepared breakfast, I asked innocently, "Are you still talking to your sister?" // Angus chewed on a buttered wad of toast. "Nope," he swallowed. // "Did you get tired of each other?" I gave him his cereal. // "Nope," he shoveled the spoon of cereal sideways into his mouth and nodded his head. "She can't anymore." // "Why is that?" I poured a cup of coffee. // "She has to get ready to be born." He slid off his chair. // I gulped and muttered, "That's reasonable." More loudly I asked, "Do you miss her?" // "Nope, we'll be talkin' soon." He ran out of the room. He didn't talk about his sister any more.

Two months flew by. Angus was adamant. He didn't want a brother. He *knew* he was going to have a sister and it was going to be a *girl*.

And so it was. We brought the tiny baby home, snuggled her into her bassinette and tiptoed out of the room. Soon we heard a clatter of toys and a low voice. We looked in and saw Angus at the bottom of her basket, his bright Matchbox cars arrayed around the bottom of her blanket. He explained, "this blue truck is for you. Now, don't break it!" He rolled the tiny vehicle up her leg and tucked it under her chin as he talked on with evident enjoyment.

The Thighs Have It

January 8th, 2009

The wistful sighs of the New Year have faded silently into oblivion. In their place, the sounds of determined laughter and giddy promises have echoed resolutely through the halls of our consciousness. The Tryst with inevitability has concluded for another year. It is time to bend over and put life to rights.

At last, the impersonal plastic containers have been packed with the stored memories of enthusiasm, excess and exhaustion. Now comes the real living.

I sighed deeply and looked down from my chair. My sighs lapsed into the reality of my thighs. There they are – very sturdy – well more than that! They appear to be uplifting, not only to my body (which needs to be carried by them) but also to me. I *knead* them daily to do what I *need* them to do – support my lifestyle.

In a fit of delayed remembrances, I think of the early years and the many ways those thighs have, in effect, held me up. Back then, modestly covered by a pleated wool skirt, my hidden limbs suggested firm curves and shapely muscles rippling down to my feet, smartly shod in gleaming, polished, high heeled pumps.

Later, in the kindergarten classroom, as the music began, thirty children hopped, skipped and galloped behind me, led by the steady clicking of my stilettos on the tiled floor. The strenuous movements flowed with ease and poise. My legs and thighs worked without conscious signals from my brain.

After class I dressed to ride the streetcar home in the late, winter afternoon. I sat on my piano bench, lifted each knee, bending them provocatively as I pulled on long, leather boots. My thighs tightened in their lithe stretch of strength and suppleness.

Now, I remember the easy movements of skiing and snow shoeing, thighs and legs gliding forward in the silent snow. Today, those thick thighs are of no apparent consequence – visually. They are scarred, swollen and inhibited from grace and the fluidity of natural mobility. Now they yearn to rest as I read, play bridge, write and yes, lie comfortably in sleep.

Still, I have tasks to do. The living room floor around me is covered with packed boxes and littered with the detritus of the season.

I place my arms behind me to raise my body from the recliner. I sigh, "Thighs, MOVE!" The muscles contract, albeit painfully. I reach for my cane and start back to work.

MARJ BEHNFELDT

*Marj was born near Deshler, Ohio, the eighth of 12 children. Marj was a
single mother raising Steven and Lisa without financial help. Her job as
a single mother to accommodate her children's schedules was as a division
manager with an educational company: hiring, training and giving classes
in 13 counties.*

*Marj became an Insurance Agent at 42, licensed in all types of insurance,
achieving Million Dollar Club in financial sales. Her primary home is in
Napoleon, Ohio. Five years ago she purchased a second home in MLG&CC
on the golf course. Marj enjoys golfing, painting, physical fitness, travel
and her family. This is Marj's first writing effort in the class on March 1st,
2012, written in approximately 30 minutes.*

Where There's Smoke There's Fire

Jason arrived home late. Gloria had held supper for him; but
she had smelled smoke on his clothes. He would have to be
more careful. The excitement was more intense with each fire.
This was the 5th house in Napoleon burned within approximately
eighteen months and people were beginning to suspect arson.

It was 9:00 a.m. when Vickie got the call at her insurance office.
Millie Reynolds house had burned last night. Vickie called it into
claims and talked with the adjuster. She decided to meet with
Fire Marshall Jack Spieless at the house at noon because arson
was suspected. Vickie visited with Millie at her daughter's house
and made sure she was comfortable. Millie was one of her favorite
clients; 80 years old, but sharp as a tack. When she met with Jack
Spieless at noon, she was astounded. The house would have to be
totaled. Although it looked like everything was in good shape and
most of the damage was in the garage; the walls were full of smoke
and since the home was brick it would be impossible to make
it livable. The smoke smell could never fully be removed from
within the walls. It was a miracle that Millie had not been killed.
Thankfully, she was working on her checkbook in the room next

to the garage and had smelled smoke. Usually, she would be fast asleep by 10:30 p.m.

Jack pointed out the car. It was totally burned. The roof of the car had caved into the body, the seats burned and it was a partial metal shell. Jack said it was a definite arson. Vickie could not believe that a basket of leaves inside the garage door, within 6 feet of the car, was totally intact, unbelievably untouched.

Vickie went back to her insurance office totally upset. This was the second large claim this year. It meant her loss ratio was in bad standing and she definitely would not qualify for a bonus this year. Oh well, she'd have to work more hours. Being a single mother with two teenagers made it hard to keep all the balls in the air. Douglas and Michelle were great at helping out and understood the long hours. Starting a new business was quite a challenge at 42; but she had perseverance and determination to succeed

Jason had decided it was time to move outside of Napoleon. People were talking; the fire department guys knew someone was starting these fires. Gloria had read the article in the paper to him and he had a difficult time not showing any emotion. The first fire outside of Napoleon was in the country. About 5 miles out, Jason thought it was an old barn. However, he had not realized that a 50 year old lady had pulled her mobile home into the barn; because the roof leaked on the house. He was horrified to learn that the lady had died in the fire. He'd have to be more careful; but he could not help himself, the compulsion was out of control. He moved to Wauseon, about 15 miles away. It wasn't far and if he went right after work he could scout out his possible targets. He was now setting at least one fire per month.

Jason had begun playing with fire as a child. That's why he had joined the fire department; but real fires happened so seldom that he had started some for the rush. It had escalated to this point and was out of control. He hated himself for this weakness; but didn't know how to stop. He knew he was sick. After the death of the lady, he hadn't started a fire for three months. He was scared. That's when he moved to Wauseon and had resumed there. Gloria was getting more and more suspicious because Jason's hours were so strange. He was gone more at night and couldn't explain the smoke and gasoline smells on his clothes, when the department had not had a fire. When she finally confronted him, he broke down and cried. He agreed to turn himself into the authorities.

Vickie was glad this sad chapter was over; but it really affected her. As a result she was required by the company to review every home policy on her books, which took a massive amount of time. Jason was tried and ended up serving a considerable amount of time in jail with extensive therapy. Many in town thought he should have received a harsher penalty with the death; but his attorney pleaded sickness and he was very fortunate in receiving 15 years with possibility of early release.

March 01, 2012

CPSIA information can be obtained at www.ICGtesting.com
Printed in the USA
LVOW102342281012

304769LV00003B/4/P

9 780985 950415